THE COWBOY
AND THE
Rose

THE COWBOY
AND THE
Rose

DENNIS NIEWOEHNER

SUNDANCE
LEGACY BOOKS

©2025 Dennis Niewoehner. All Rights Reserved.

No part of this book may be reproduced, stored in a retrieval system, or transmitted in any form or by any means—electronic, mechanical, photocopying, recording, or otherwise—without the prior written permission of the publisher, except in the case of brief quotations embodied in critical reviews and certain other noncommercial uses permitted by copyright law.

This is a work of fiction. Names, characters, places, and incidents are either the product of the author's imagination or used fictitiously. Any resemblance to actual persons, living or dead, or actual events is purely coincidental. While real locations may be referenced, they are used in a fictional manner and should not be considered accurate depictions of those areas.

Published by Sundance Legacy Books, LLC

SUNDANCE
LEGACY BOOKS

Hardcover: 979-8-9927876-1-0
Hardcover w/DJ: 979-8-9927876-2-7
Paperback: 979-8-9927876-3-4
Audiobook: 979-8-9927876-4-1
Kindle: 979-8-9927876-5-8

Library of Congress Cataloging Number 2025904150
Cataloging-in-Publication data on file with the publisher.

Cover illustration by Jay Moore, www.JayMooreStudio.com
Publishing services by Concierge Marketing Inc.

Printed in the United States of America
10 9 8 7 6 5 4 3 2

★

WHO IS DENNIS NIEWOEHNER?
BY JEROME RYDEN

DENNIS NIEWOEHNER is a superb storyteller. After a successful business career and a lifetime of community service, Dennis has been writing self-help books for seniors and personal stories of his life and family history to pass on to his grandchildren. I feel his latest book, *The Cowboy and the Rose*, has the potential to be on the national bestseller list.

At the 2000 Cornerstone Award ceremony in Parker, Colorado, Dennis's previous real estate partner, Jim Nicholson, who later served as Ambassador to the Vatican and the secretary of veterans' affairs under President George W. Bush, said, "There are people who hold that man and development must ever live in conflict with nature. That there is no way for the two to live peaceably together and for both to flourish. Dennis, you prove the opposite, although I don't think you set out to prove anything."

Tell me the facts and I'll learn.
Tell me the truth and I'll believe.
But tell me a story and it will live
in my heart forever!

~ Native American Proverb ~

DEDICATION

I would like to dedicate this book to Robert James Waller:

The respect I had for Waller stems from my admiration of his diverse interests in life. He affected my life in a deeply inspirational way, proving that one can master many fields with determination and passion. From academia to fiction writing, his achievements inspired me to pursue excellence across my own endeavors.

~ Robert James Waller ~
1939 to 2017

Elinor C. Perry was my mother-in-law and one of my best friends in life. She always encouraged me and was so proud of my accomplishments. She exemplified the phrase "I Am Woman": brilliant and sophisticated, yet humble with an understanding and forgiving heart.

She loved the manuscript but died before I finished writing Chapter 28. I finished writing this chapter when Callie's words of wisdom and inspiration came to me through Elly's spirit.

~ Elinor C. Perry ~
1918 - 2021

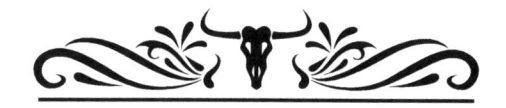

FOREWORD

Dennis Niewoehner and I connected through an uncommon love of Douglas County's hardscrabble history and majestic landscape. An incurable romantic about all thing's "cowboy," he was well into his dream of writing a bestseller. Such things are long shots, especially for old-timers. But he had magic under his saddle . . .

I'm told it was a starry September night over a Plum Creek campfire when Dennis' friend and fellow rancher poured out his life of love and sorrows. So moving was his story that Dennis knew instantly it was the missing piece to his own odyssey.

Ironic, really, that a bit of moonlight and a few mugs of coffee unlocked the serpentine journey of a life so richly lived.

The Cowboy and the Rose is the novelization of an agonizing love story, epitomizing how love creates both happiness and sadness in our lives. Take it to heart and you will fully understand your own capacity for gentleness and hope.

The book is principally about fate and how to deal with it: by taking the good with the bad and accepting responsibility for one's mistakes.

That fate cannot be halted but only slowed and shaped.

Yesterday is history; today is the future. Here in Douglas County, Colorado, we deal with these things by "cowboying up": making the best of difficult situations and then finding a new trail.

A bonus within this unforgettable romance is its Western backdrop, unfolding as it does within the magnificent, awe-inspiring beauty of the Plum Creek Basin, where buffalo do roam, deer and antelope abound, and the skies are almost always blue and go on forever. In these parts, lives are no different from others: riddled with triumphs, sorrows, and much in between. How we react to our todays makes all the difference in our tomorrows.

This saga shows the possibilities in the world of human relationships.

Like Garth Brooks songs with lyrics that drive our emotions, allowing us to feel and relate.

To understand this story, readers must enter a world of gentleness and just perhaps, find themselves there as well.

Like *The Bridges of Madison County*, *The Cowboy and the Rose* will stay with you forever.

Like the sound of a meadowlark on a warm summer's eve.

~Joe Gschwendtner

INTRODUCTION

The story I am about to tell is one that I felt compelled to write. I heard it for the first time while I was working on a book titled *Backstory*. To gather material for my book, I interviewed people who told me their backstories and reflected on turning points in their lives.

One interview with a successful rancher from Douglas County, Colorado, stood out from the rest. Why? Because it included the most touching love story I'd encountered since reading *The Bridges of Madison County* by Robert James Waller. Immediately I felt compelled to share this beautiful yet sad love story with the world.

In the process of retelling this story, I added a little of my own imagination to smooth out the rough edges of the narrative and supply some missing details. Although my rancher friend is well educated, he's a man of few words.

And the interview started . . .

"Dennis, it was such a pleasure talking to you. It has been an interesting couple of days tracing the path my life has taken. However, I did not tell you everything.

"Last night, I could not sleep. I tossed and turned for hours trying to decide whether I should tell you another story—a story that has made me very happy but comes with a lot of sadness. I finally decided that I need to tell this story. I am hoping it will relieve some of my pain and sadness if I have a chance to talk it out; however, I need you to honor our confidentiality agreement and not use my name or her name. Let's use the names Remington (Rem for short) Cunningham for me and Callie Rose Parker for her.

"As I tell you my story, I think we need to have Callie tell her story at the same time. You're probably thinking, 'How can she do that?' With your solemn promise to return it to me, let me give you Callie's personal journal. I will tell you later how I was able to get the journal. As you know, every story has two sides. Callie's journal will describe what took place from her point of view."

Nodding solemnly, I responded, "You have my assurance that I will never reveal your name or her name to anyone. You and I have signed a legally binding confidentiality agreement to that effect. And of course I would never betray our friendship."

With a nod, my friend began talking.

"It all started during the spring of 1999. I was in the middle of training roping horses and I needed some extra help on the ranch."

My friend recounted his story over the next few days as we hung around the barn, walked down to the Cottonwood grove, or sat with a cup of coffee in the big leather chairs inside his ranch house.

CHAPTER 1
REMINGTON CUNNINGHAM

With his saddle hoisted over his right shoulder, Rem walked along the fence line. Gazing at the early-morning Colorado blue sky, he relished the natural beauty of life in the country. His nose caught the dewy, fresh scent of damp soil and earth that only early morning air could provide. The rising sun lit the valley, spreading a golden glow that climbed up the two buttes southwest of the ranch. Two hawks circled with the wind currents, appearing to be sailing rather than flying. Everything seemed calm and beautiful now, but the forecast called for intense storms later in the afternoon.

Rem smiled as he heard the familiar nicker of Cimarron, the eight-year-old red sorrel quarter horse gelding he had raised and trained since he was a foal. Not only was Cimarron a highly ranked roping horse and Rem's favorite, but he caught everyone's attention with his four white stockings, long red mane, and stunning tail.

After Rem's morning ride on Cimarron, he intended to cover the haystack by the barn with a tarp and move the tractor inside. Rain would be welcome, but he hoped hail wouldn't accompany it. His first cutting of alfalfa hay looked good; it would be a shame to lose it to bad weather now. After a long and challenging winter and a very wet spring, today's sunshine felt warm and welcoming.

As Rem's eyes traced the landscape, he reflected on his father's wisdom in moving the family from Washington, D.C., to Douglas County, Colorado, when Rem and his brother were boys.

Leaving Washington for Colorado had been an easy transition, since Rem was only seven when they moved. Rem had looked at maps of the United States in school but had no idea how big the country really was until they drove to Colorado. During that long car trip through the heartland, he realized how much he liked horses, especially when he saw them galloping across open fields along the interstate highway.

When the family stopped for food and gas in North Platte, Nebraska, young Rem wandered over to an adjoining pasture to watch a herd drinking from a galvanized watering tank. He approached the fence line slowly, and a few of the horses extended their heads to be petted on the nose and to have their ears scratched.

Walking away to join his family for lunch, Rem relished the smell of the horses on his hands. He loved the scent so much that he decided not to wash his hands before lunch.

When the food arrived at the table, Rem asked his dad, "Can I get a horse when we move to our new ranch?"

Rem's father smiled and said, "You bet! In fact, I'm thinking we need to get more than one horse."

When they returned to the car, Rem leaned into the front seat and whispered, "I can't wait until we get there. Would you like to smell my hands from petting the horses? Isn't it just the greatest smell?"

After Robert had attended the aeronautical conferences at the Air Force Academy on the north side of Colorado Springs, the choice to move his family to Colorado had been easy. For Rem's father, Douglas County represented everything he needed for himself and his family. It would take them away from the heavy traffic and overcrowding of Washington. D.C. He looked forward to getting away from the politics associated with the government.

Robert also found that Douglas County wasn't just beautiful. The area offered resources for families and business, with high quality education and extracurricular activities. It was close to both Denver and Colorado Springs, with easy access to parks, trails, and open spaces. For work, the area had an energetic economic environment and a lot of business opportunity. It was perfect for raising a happy family.

As he recalled those long-ago times, Rem stumbled on the saddle's leather cinch strap that was dragging along the ground. Bending over, he picked it up and tossed it over the saddle horn.

Rem's mind was distracted by thoughts of his brother Wade's betrayal after their father's passing. He kept racking his brain, struggling to comprehend how his brother could have done something so hurtful. At least his father would never know what his other son had done to Rem and the family's three ranches.

Rem had nearly been pushed to the brink by their father's unexpected passing, the trauma of that day forever embedded in his memory.

Rem had found his dad in the barn, slumped over a bale of hay he had been carrying to a horse stall. After desperately checking for a pulse or heartbeat, Rem called 911. His hands trembled as he dialed, his voice cracking as he described the situation to the operator. Overwhelmed, he collapsed over his father, tears soaking his cheek as he clung tightly to him. He could not imagine life without his dad in it. The only solace he found was in the thought that his father would have wanted to be in his barn, wearing his leather gloves and cowboy boots, during his final moments. Rem had not only lost his dad, but he had also lost his best friend and lifetime hero.

Ever since Rem was a small boy learning to ride a horse, he and his dad had been thick as thieves. Even as a teenager, Rem spent most of his time with his dad down at the barn working with the horses. After a long day of exercising the horses, they would lead all the horses into their stalls to feed them hay and their ration of grain.

At day's end, the sounds and smells inside the barn soothed the soul and lowered the day's stress to a level that made them feel as if all was right with the world. Listening to the horses eat and whinny in delight, Robert and Rem would turn off the lights and close the big sliding barn door behind them. As they walked together towards the house, their conversations would range from what they were planning to have for dinner to far deeper subjects.

Rem's love and admiration for his father was evident. He looked up to him, aspiring to accomplish all that his father had achieved in life and more.

While they were walking to the house one evening, Rem said, "Dad, I know you flew many missions during the war, but why don't you ever talk about it and tell me what happened?"

His dad stopped walking, looked up at the evening sky, and quietly said, "Son, let's sit on the fence over here for just a minute."

As they sat next to each other on the fence, Robert said to Rem, "Tonight I will tell you about the war, but it will be the only time I will speak of the war and my missions. I did what I had to do for America, but that part of my life is over and will be recorded in the history books.

"I was the captain of a B-17 whose mission was to fly out of Great Britain loaded with bombs to drop on the industrial cities of Germany. I flew many missions; often, my plane limped back to our landing strip outside of London with an engine that was not running well and a hull and wings riddled with bullets from German anti-aircraft guns.

"After making an emergency landing, the most difficult thing to do was check on our gunners, who were strapped into their glass cages with machine guns to shoot at enemy fighter planes. On multiple occasions, I had to call the medics to cut them out of their harnesses so they could be treated. Since a flight crew is very closely knit, my heart broke when I would find one of them dead."

"As the captain, it was my job to write a letter to their wives or mothers explaining how their loved one had died. Before each mission, each soldier passed me a letter with the address on the envelope. With my letter included, I would pass the stack of letters to the ground crew chief in case the bomber did not return."

With tears in his eyes, Robert said, "Rem, I helped carry nine bodies off the plane, and I wrote nine letters to their families. I know you think I am strong, but after writing each letter I sobbed like a baby. I still say a prayer for each of my men every night so I will never forget them; however, that is my burden to carry, not yours. You deserved to hear this story since it has been on your mind. We will never speak about it again... agreed?"

With a lump in his throat, Rem responded quietly.

"Dad, thank you for sharing that with me. I will never bring it up again, as you asked. In case I never get a chance to tell you, I have always loved you, but now I know another part of who my dad is, and I love and admire you more than ever."

Not only had his dad been a highly successful military pilot and aeronautics pioneer, but he was also a true gentleman—one of the best Rem had ever known. He displayed his gentle nature in every aspect of his life, whether it was as a husband to his wife, a father to his two sons, or a trainer of the horses on the ranch. He had grit and a good head on his shoulders, always knowing the right words to say when the going got tough. In other words, he was a tried-and-true cowboy.

Later that evening, as the boys were washing the dinner dishes, Robert motioned for his wife, Barbara, to follow him into the study. As she walked next to him, he smiled as he remembered all the things he loved about her. She was not only beautiful but a very brave woman who faced problems straight on. Her soft-spoken voice was the icing on the cake.

Taking her hands in his, he whispered near her ear, "Barb, I just told Rem about my missions in the B-17 and about how many men I lost."

Robert paused. "I didn't mention David. If you agree, I feel that it's time we tell the boys what happened to Wade's father, and the truth about how you and I got together."

Barbara's eyes welled up with tears. Upon seeing her reaction, Robert forced himself to take a deep breath before continuing. "Wade has always known I adopted him and that you are his real mother. It's time he knew who his birth father was and how he died. The boys know that he died before you and I were married, but this wouldn't be the first time Rem has asked me about Wade's biological father." Nodding, Barbara spoke resolutely. "It is time, and even though this will be hard on Wade, we need to do it. Let me make some coffee and cocoa, and then have the boys join us in the living room."

As Robert turned to go, Barbara caught his arm. "Would you do the talking? This will be difficult for Wade, so please don't be upset if he leaves the room. If he does, I will go to him."

Quietly, she added, "I love you, Robert."

After everyone sat down, Robert looked at both teenagers and said, "I have a story to tell you, and if either of you starts to cry—or if we all do—it will be okay."

Rem and Wade gave Robert a puzzled look, but he continued. "While we were walking up from the barn, I told Rem about my many flight missions over Germany in my B-17 bomber during World War II. We lost many men on our different missions when our plane was riddled by bullets from anti-aircraft guns. That being said, there is one story that needs to be shared with both of you.

"On what was to be my last mission, my co-pilot—my best friend David—was hit by enemy fire and died as we flew back to England. After our plane landed, as the captain, I received the required "If I don't return" letter from our ground crew so I could send it to David's wife. We all had to write such a letter in case the airplane never returned.

"Since I was leaving for the United States the next day, I decided to accompany the body of my best friend on the flight and take the letter with me so I could give it to his wife.

"When I arrived at her house and passed her the letter announcing he had died, I was quick to spot a little boy holding onto her leg. He looked up at me with huge, questioning eyes as his mom sobbed, the tears rolling down her face. Steadying him so he would not fall, I leaned over and picked him up so I could hold him close to me. He was so brave."

Robert paused to gather himself, then continued, "He did not cry even though a stranger was holding him. Instead, he touched my face and laid his head on my shoulder. Wade, that courageous little boy was you."

Robert paused, allowing Wade time to respond if he wanted to. Wade's shoulders were tense, his lips sealed tightly as his eyes connected with his father's. It was apparent that he had nothing to say yet, so Robert continued.

"Since David had been my best friend, I stayed for the funeral and a few days afterward to help your mom get her affairs in order. During that time, you and I became the best of friends, Wade.

"Over the course of the next year, your mom and I corresponded through letters and I paid a few visits to see both of you. Your mom and I discovered that we loved each other, and we decided to get married. A year later, Rem was born. We felt very blessed having the two of you."

Concerned, Barbara turned to Wade and asked, "Honey, are you doing okay? Is there anything you want to ask your dad or me? You've been so quiet."

Noticing that Wade was shaking a little, Rem slid closer to him on the couch and put his hand on his brother's shoulder. Quietly, he spoke. "I'm so sorry, Wade. You know we love you."- Looking up at Robert, his voice quivering, Wade asked, "Dad, was my real father a hero?"

Robert knelt beside his son and clasped his hand. "Son, your father was one of the bravest men I have ever known. When many of us were scared during these missions, he was a strong soldier who would assure all of us that we were going to be okay. To this day, I still consider him my best friend, and I pray for him every night."

The room fell silent as Wade rose from his seat. "I think I would like to go to my room now," he said, turning to leave. He paused as he made his way across the room, glancing back at his family.

"Thank you for telling me who my father was. I am very proud of him."

CHAPTER 2
ROSE CALLIE PARKER

As Callie laced her jogging shoes, loneliness covered her, heavy and suffocating. Bill's presence felt like a ghost, a constant reminder of his emotional absence. She moved to the window, arms wrapped tightly around herself, watching him back out of the driveway. He didn't even glance her way this time; his half-hearted wave felt like a cruel reminder of how little he seemed to care.

Her loneliness gnawed at her, but beneath it simmered a quiet fury she could no longer ignore. How could she always feel so completely alone even when her husband was right there? The thought simmered as his car disappeared down the street, leaving her with nothing but silence—and the growing fury that she had let herself settle for so little.

Bill was a renowned cardiologist who traveled around the country every week giving seminars on open-heart surgery. It was common for him to be gone for days or weeks each month. Callie's sadness and frustration was not due to her husband leaving on yet another business trip. Instead, she was feeling the aftershocks of a fight they'd had just a few hours earlier.

Desperate for something—anything—that might catch Bill's attention, Callie tiptoed into his study wearing nothing but a trench coat. She had rehearsed this moment in her mind, clinging to the hope that it might rekindle something between them, not that the flame was ever that hot.

With her heart pounding, she leaned against the doorframe and slowly opened the coat, her smile trembling awkwardly as she tried to sound playful. "I have a snack for you," she said, her voice tinged with both nerves and longing, expecting rejection, but trying anyway.

Bill barely tilted his chin up, his eyes still fixed on his computer screen. "Grab that medical manual over there," he asked, his tone flat and dismissive. After a pause, he added without even glancing her way, "And while you're at it, a beer would be the real snack. Go put some clothes on and read a book or something."

Callie stood frozen, the weight of his indifference crashing over her. Her forced smile faded, and she clutched the edges of the coat, suddenly wishing she could disappear.

Mortified, Callie stormed out of the study and fled to their bedroom. Later, when Bill finally came to bed, she was still awake but didn't say a word. She had been thinking about how Bill always found ways to make her feel like a desperate, pathetic fool.

Just last week he'd said to her, "What do you even do all day? You have a college degree—you graduated cum laude—and for what? Are you just lazy?"

Callie shot back angrily, "With you gone all the time, who do you think runs this household? You don't understand anything, and you have no right to talk to me that way!"

Their words hung heavily between them as he made no apology, turning and angrily walking out the door.

Callie and Bill had been married for almost 22 years. Two of their three boys were in college, and the youngest was in officer's training school for the army in Ft. Benning, Georgia. Callie could never quite rid herself of the loneliness that caused her to wonder, *Is this really all there is? How does a cardiologist not have a heart of his own?*

What bothered Callie most was remembering that she had felt the same loneliness when she was a young bride. Had she been expecting too much? She always knew she had made a huge mistake marrying Bill, but she also knew that she had obligations to the kids.

As she sat at the kitchen table sipping coffee, Callie reflected on her childhood.

Her sister, Beth, and she were very different but had always been close. With Callie being the prettier of the two, there was friction between the girls. Beth had done very well academically, and since they both studied intensely to achieve good grades, there was little time to go out with friends. That changed in high school when Callie came into her own, winning the title of Prom Queen during her senior year. Soon afterward, she started going steady with Steve, the school's track star.

Thinking back, she realized her feelings of loneliness had started soon after she began dating Steve. At first their relationship was exciting, but she felt like being the high school's star couple was altering Steve's behavior around her. Under constant pressure from Steve, she finally slept with him a week before graduation. The next day, she discovered from her girlfriends that Steve bragged to his buddies that he had "not only nailed her, but nailed her good" and that he was looking forward to going to college and making more conquests. Ashamed and embarrassed, Callie did not date during the rest of the summer, and she avoided her former friends. Feeling isolated and lonely, she left for college in September.

At college she dated rarely until the middle of her junior year when she met her husband-to-be, Bill. He was a very intense and hard-working student who needed to maintain a high grade point average to earn a scholarship for medical school.

Just as Callie was starting to feel a small sense of security in their relationship, Bill proposed at the end of their senior year. "Cal, you know, it would help me out if we could just get married, get it over with, and move on," he said, his words more practical than heartfelt. Saying yes felt like the right thing to do at the time, but Callie realized too late that she had fallen into the habit of doing what was expected instead of stopping to think—let alone feel.

Callie didn't think she had ever been in love, so she was unsure of how love would feel. Being a romantic at heart, Callie wondered if there was a certain feeling that came over a person or if they could love someone without being in love. She also wondered if Bill was even in love with her. Maybe he just wanted her to work to support him while he was in medical school. With Bill always studying, they didn't have much private time together. He was always too tired to have sex, so their intimacy slowly faded away.

Feeling lost and rejected, Callie joined an exercise club with two of her girlfriends. There, she met Dave, the manager of the club. As she and Dave got to know each other, she started to develop feelings that she had never known before. Was this what love actually felt like, or was it just sexual attraction? Either way, she was determined to find out.

One evening after class, Callie and Dave went out for drinks at the local neighborhood pub. After drinking more than usual, Callie stumbled back to the club with Dave, who told her that he needed to get his car keys from his office. After they walked into his office, he closed the door and kissed her very passionately. Lonely and intoxicated, she kissed him back and wrapped her legs around his waist. Given that opening, he proceeded to make love to her on the floor.

A few days later, Callie found out that Dave was married. Confused and hurt, she confronted him after her next class and asked if they could meet in private.

"Callie," Dave replied with a smile, "Yes, let's go to my office."

Dave closed the door after Callie entered and approached her from behind. Immediately, Callie turned and slapped his face as she yelled, "I can't believe you are married and took advantage of my vulnerability!"

As she stood before him, anger boiling under her skin, she wondered how she had ever fallen for his charm. Had she been that desperate for connection? That starved for affection?

"Now, wait a minute, Callie—I..." Dave stuttered before she cut him off.

"You have no right to talk here. I would call your wife, but I don't want her to be hurt. I have thought about this for a few

days, and I feel like you should resign as the manager of this club. Your behavior toward me was unacceptable!"

She wiped tears from her cheeks as she continued talking.

"My best friend Helen is also in your class, and her husband is one of the owners. If you get fired, your career is over! So, I guess I will hear that you resigned when I come for my next class." She sighed heavily, searching Dave's eyes for a response. *"I really liked you, Dave, and I can't believe you did this to me. You really hurt me."*

With that, she swiftly left the room, leaving Dave to stand alone in silence, the weight of her pain lingering in the air.

She quit the class later that day.

A few months later, Callie discovered she was pregnant. With a sense of dread, she realized that the baby's father might be Dave instead of Bill. Knowing this, she told Bill she was pregnant and that they should get married without delay. Not only was he upset that she was pregnant, but he was irritated that she would have to stay home to take care of a baby instead of working while he was in medical school.

Callie shook her head and straightened her shoulders as she attempted to bring her focus back to the present. Her coffee had turned cold, so she set the cup down, wondering what was wrong with her. She needed to forget the past. To the outside world her life appeared to be perfect. As far as everyone else could see, Bill provided a good living for the family. All three children had excelled in school and sports. Her life felt full, yet her heart was completely empty.

CHAPTER 3
A FATHER TO BE PROUD OF

Rem's dad, Robert, kept himself in excellent physical shape. In middle age and beyond, he felt proud when people mentioned how fit and trim he was. Despite the compliments, he knew that he should use common sense and not exert himself by doing too much ranch work.

He would always tell people, "I don't worry about getting older; everybody gets older. Just remember, we always have today." He would smile humbly and say, "Today is cash, yesterday is a canceled check, and tomorrow is a promissory note. You need to live large and make the most of every opportunity."

As his father aged, Rem would sometimes find Robert sitting alone among the cottonwood trees, looking out at the valley. When Rem walked over to join him, his dad often had tears in his eyes. Robert never told Rem the secret that tormented his soul. It was something he had never shared with anyone, including Barbara. The guilt had weighed on him ever since Wade's father died in their last mission together. The grueling internal debate over whether he should take his guilt to the grave with him or tell Wade the real story of how David had died and how Robert was involved had plagued his mind for years. Perhaps the time to come clean had finally arrived.

Before becoming a rancher, Rem's dad had been one of the most prominent people in the aviation field in the United States. After graduating from Yale University, he entered Army flight school and then became a highly decorated pilot in the U.S. Army Air Force during World War II. After the war, he flew as a commercial pilot for Pan American Airways.

During the 1950s, he served as an advisor to the FAA and NASA. He had received the Wright Brothers Master Pilot Award and the FAA's Distinguished Achievement Award. Robert's exemplary service had caught the president's attention, and a cabinet-level position was under consideration.

Before accepting the offer, Robert wanted to discuss his next move with Barbara. Now that they had two young boys to raise, decision making had become much more complicated.

One evening, after entering the house and setting his briefcase down in the hallway, Robert called out to Barbara, "Honey, if you are not too busy in the kitchen, could you come into my study?"

"Sure, give me a second and I will be right in," she responded. "Would you like a glass of wine?"

As Barbara sat across from him on the other side of his desk, Robert told her about the position that might be offered to him by the president. Meeting her gaze, he asked softly, "Honey, what is your dream for the next stage of our life together?"

Looking down at her hands, she spoke softly. "Thanks for thinking of me. I have been wanting to talk to you about this. Now that your career has reached this point, we need to focus on guiding our two boys down a new path. I know you love Colorado, and I have fond memories of my parents' cabin in Evergreen, Colorado. I would love to move there so we could raise these boys somewhere other than Washington D.C."

"Honey, I'm totally on board, and I can't wait for this next part of our life together." Robert smiled and gave her an enthusiastic hug.

When Barbara was diagnosed with colon cancer at age 36, Robert felt the pull of Colorado even more deeply. Wanting to spend as much time as possible with her and their two young sons, he resigned his positions in Washington D.C. and moved the family to Colorado. He felt the ranching lifestyle would benefit the boys, especially if Barbara didn't recover.

Douglas County had always captured Robert's heart. During his time in New York City and then Washington D.C., Robert's horizons were initially limited by the demands of his increasingly responsible positions. That changed when he began traveling to Colorado to teach and consult for what was then the cutting edge of astronautic science at the Air Force Academy.

During Robert's visits to Colorado, he felt as if he had been born again. Every time he arrived, he reveled in the openness, vast blue skies, and refreshing weather.

The topography of mountains, buttes, and prairies north of the Palmer Divide seemed exquisite to Robert. It was like nothing he had ever seen before, ranging from lush valleys of prairie grass to massive cottonwood trees, intermittent streams, and red rock formations. Mesas, arroyos, rolling meadows, and buttes stood as sentinels overseeing a land once deemed sacred by the Ute, Cheyenne, and Arapaho tribes.

For Robert, the expansive Divide Plateau offered a spiritual harmony with the massive mountains behind it. He also learned that Colorado weather would allow him to view the panoramic majesty of Pike's Peak in Colorado Springs to Longs Peak for all but 60 days annually. Though not deeply religious, he often described the area as "a painting straight from God's palette."

Then there was Highway 105 that paralleled Plum Creek, running the length of the valley from Sedalia to Palmer Lake. Robert felt that, in its own way, it was as strikingly beautiful as Highway 1 on the California Coast. It was in this basin that Robert bought his first ranch.

Years later, he acquired another smaller ranch near Sedalia, and a few months after, a third ranch south of

Greenland. The Greenland ranch was irrigated to ensure a supply of oats and hay under drought conditions.

As the years passed, Robert grew to enjoy ranching more and more. Barbara seemed to be holding her own in her battle with cancer. She received excellent treatment at Fitzsimmons Hospital in Denver. Since it was a military hospital, she was able to see many of their old friends from the Air Corps, which helped keep her spirits high. Since Robert was still highly regarded in the aeronautics field, he was visited by many leaders in the aviation industry, as well as congressmen and senators who jockeyed for his support. He felt honored when two highly decorated fighter pilots visited the ranch for their family holiday.

Even though he enjoyed these visits, Robert would always tell Rem that what he enjoyed most was putting some of those city slickers on horseback. He would pick horses that he could trust and take the men for a trail ride around the rugged buttes and down into the dry arroyos. At the end of the day, many of them were as happy as little boys who had always wanted to be cowboys. Others were so terrified after the ride that they immediately headed for the bar, which was conveniently set up in the barn.

After all the guests had left, Robert would saddle up his horse and take a slow, relaxing ride around the hay meadows and outlying pastures. He would reflect on all the conversations he'd had with his friends, remembering the good and bad news he'd heard.

Gazing at the beauty of the ranch and the surrounding buttes and mesas, he knew he had made the right move for the family. He hoped that his hard work would be carried on by the two boys running the three ranches, preserving his legacy for generations to come.

> As an admirer of the western history of Douglas County, Robert found that his secondary purchase spoke to him like no other. Every time he drove into the front gate, he felt as though he had gone back in time. The ranch, named "Pretty Woman Ranch," was owned by Sylvestor and Elizabeth Richardson.
>
> Elizabeth was proclaimed by political travelers and Indian scouts to be the prettiest woman in all territorial Colorado. The most famous visitor of all was Kit Carson, who made his last campfire in May 1868 very near Pretty Woman Ranch. Transported in the back of a horse-drawn wagon, he died two days later in Fort Garland on his way home to die in Taos, New Mexico. One week later, Elizabeth divorced her husband and moved back to Sheboygan, Wisconsin, with her eight-year-old son Denver. What had caused this sudden move and long prairie trip back to Wisconsin? Some have speculated that Elizabeth's decision was connected to knowing that Kit had died and believing there was no reason to stay with Sylvestor in Colorado.

Fitzsimmons Hospital's rich history included providing care to famous visitors. It was the same hospital that treated President Dwight D. Eisenhower when he had a heart attack in Denver. President Eisenhower had spent a considerable amount of time in Colorado due to the fact that his wife Mamie's parents lived in Denver.

CHAPTER 4
A GROWING RIFT

Rem would never forget that Christmas morning when he was eight years old.

Rem and his brother, Wade, were opening Christmas presents, and it turned out that Wade had received one more present than Rem. Suddenly, their dad looked at Rem and said, "Let's walk down to the barn together." Rem jumped up and down in excitement as they put on their winter coats and rubber boots. "Hurry, Dad," he exclaimed. "I can't wait another minute!"

When they arrived at the barn, his dad pushed open the heavy sliding door to the horse stall area. Standing right before them was the most beautiful black pony Rem had ever seen. Tied on top of the black pony's halter was a red bow. Rem approached the pony very slowly, a big grin on his face. He quickly threw his arms around the pony's neck and looked back at his dad.

"Thanks, Dad," he said appreciatively. "This is the best Christmas present ever! I only want one other thing when I'm older." His dad asked, "Well, what would that be, son?" Rem replied, "Someday, when I grow up, I want to be just like you!"

As Rem grew, he listened to his dad's stories and advice like it was gospel. In contrast, Wade would often walk away from conversations or argue until a discussion had escalated into a serious confrontation.

One day, down at the barn, Rem found Wade sitting on a hay bale instead of feeding the horses. In a louder voice than necessary, Rem looked at Wade and said, "What is your problem? You don't want to do any work around the ranch, and you are so rude to Dad. I'm tired of it. It upsets Mom to the point of tears. Do you think you're the center of the universe?"

Wade slapped his hands on his knees as he stood up, spat, and replied, "Rem, do you really want to know what is bothering me, or are you just doing your typical good boy complaining? You want an answer? Well, I'll give you an answer.

"You have been bothering me for years. Your close friendship with Dad is sickening, and you are such a suck-up. You don't treat me like an equal or a brother. You and I are supposed to be buddies, but instead it's always you and Dad! I'm on the outside, and if it wasn't for Mom, I would have been out of here years ago!"

As Wade stormed away, a flicker of regret crossed his mind, but it was quickly buried under years of resentment and the gnawing belief that he would always live in Rem's shadow. No matter how hard he tried, the bond between Rem and their father always seemed unshakable—a constant reminder of everything Wade felt he lacked.

Rem moved to follow, but Wade spun around and shoved him hard. Rem stumbled back, his head slamming into the stall door.

"Get out of my face and go play with your horses, Rem. Just leave me alone and let me enjoy doing what I like to do. If you can't accept it, then at least give me the opportunity to kick your ass. You know I can, but then you will have to explain to Dad that you fell off a horse."

★

Later, Robert took Wade on a long horseback ride and told him why he had felt responsible for David's death. Robert begged Wade never to reveal the story to anyone. Wade agreed, with the caveat that Robert would never call him "son" again. As a caring father, Robert had hoped and prayed that this gesture might help to heal their relationship. Instead, it pushed them farther apart.

Before traveling to Europe, Robert entrusted Wade with a General Power of Attorney, a document meant to authorize Wade to sign papers on Robert's behalf during his absence. However, unbeknownst to Robert, Wade altered the document's expiration date, extending its validity well beyond the intended timeframe. Instead of allowing it to expire upon Robert's return to Colorado, Wade secretly stored the revised document in a safe deposit box, intending to keep it as leverage for future use. This act of deception planted the seeds for the betrayal that would eventually unravel the family's trust.

Wade's disdain for ranching was evident from a young age. He detested chores and showed no interest in raising or riding horses, often shirking responsibilities whenever possible. As a teenager, he worked during the summer on the family's ranches but usually showed up late for work and left early. This was the first of many issues that would lead to arguments with their dad and widen the rift between the brothers. Even though the family had three ranches to look after, Robert had always told the boys that they could pick any career field that suited them. Wade made his disdain for ranching very clear when given the chance.

Wade and Rem, two years apart in age, had been the best of friends as little boys. As they grew older their interests changed, causing them to grow apart—so much so that at times they hated each other.

The fight in the barn left a mark—both physical and emotional. Rem stumbled backward, his face stinging and warm with blood, as Wade stormed off, his anger as raw as the cut on Rem's cheek. From that day on, the brothers avoided each other like strangers, their bond fractured beyond repair.

CHAPTER 5
LIFE CHANGED

Barbara's cancer treatments were very effective for almost five years. It appeared that she was winning the battle and would not need to go through another colorectal surgery. She appeared to be on the road to recovery, but Barbara's battle was far from over.

One day around feeding time, Rem found his dad alone in the tack room, sobbing uncontrollably. He had never seen his dad cry before. It was difficult to see such a stoic figure with tears streaming down his cheeks; in all honesty, it scared Rem to death.

He hugged his dad and asked him what was wrong. Robert collapsed into a chair and blurted out, "I just received a call from your mom's doctor. The most recent tests show that the cancer has spread to her brain and her bones. The doctor wants us to meet with him tomorrow morning to hear the news together."

Stunned, Rem listened as his father explained, "I can't face her right now. Would you call up to the house and tell

Mom and Wade that you and I need to go to Denver? Tell her it's to meet with the Board of the National Western Stock Show regarding the roping agenda for next year and not to wait up for us because it will be late when we get home. I'm sorry to make you do this, but I can't deal with it."

"Of course, Dad, whatever you need." Rem agreed. "Hop in the pickup when you're ready to go and I will be out in a minute."

In silence, they drove to the Castle Rock Ranch and then on to the Old Stone Church restaurant to get a bite to eat. They barely spoke as the day went on, spending the time quietly grieving for what was to come. Before returning to the ranch around midnight, they drove up to Round Top Mountain to say a prayer. They knelt on the rugged rocks and gazed at the full moon, which was starting to descend toward the snow-covered peaks of the Continental Divide.

The tranquility of the setting added to the somber gravity of Robert and Rem's realization that Barbara was dying. Holding hands, they silently walked back to Robert's pickup as morning approached.

The next day, Robert told Barbara that the doctor had called requesting a visit with them that morning. After they met with the doctor, Barbara was hospitalized and brought into the hospice program.

Knowing that she was approaching the end of her life, Barbara asked each of her three men to come into her room alone. She drew a shallow breath as Robert stepped into the room. Barbara extended her hand, beckoning Robert to join her at her bedside. He was quick to move towards her, clasping her frail hand in the warmth of his own.

Fighting for strength, she leaned toward him and whispered, "Robert, I hate leaving you, but I want you to know that I am at peace. You provided me with a life that I dreamed about as a little girl, and I will be forever grateful for that. Hurry, now, and send Wade in."

Back in the hallway, Robert looked at Wade. "Mom wants to see you now."

As Wade entered, Barbara struggled to find the energy to speak. Looking up at Wade, she said, "Honey, you and I have always been so close. Please know that you have filled my heart with so much joy, and every day you've reminded me just how lucky I am to be your mother. I love you so much, more than you'll ever know." With tears in her eyes she asked, "Could you hurry and get Rem for me?"

As Rem entered, Barbara looked at him, her eyes struggling to stay open. With her voice barely above a whisper, she said, "Remington, you are so strong, and I've always been so proud of you. Promise me you'll look after Wade. He's a gentle soul, but he's lost, and he'll need your guidance more than ever. You're the anchor of this family now. I love you."

The night Barbara took her last breath, a deafening silence fell over Robert, Wade, and Rem. Not a word was spoken during the long ride back to the ranch, and the silence continued when they arrived home, and his sons lingered, weeping in the car. Robert knew that nothing he could say would soften the harsh reality that their mother was forever gone from the world.

The funeral at the church in Castle Rock was sad yet stately. It also happened to be the largest funeral the little town of Castle Rock had ever seen. Not only did congressmen and senators come to pay their respects, but Robert was consoled by the wife of a fighter pilot who had served in Korea.

Rem would never forget the eulogy provided by the visiting priest from St. John's Episcopal Church in Washington, D.C. After talking about Barbara's fortitude in fighting cancer, he walked into the congregation with his handheld microphone. Fixing his gaze on the people in the front row, he told a story that held everyone's attention.

"As an elderly priest who is getting ready to retire, and with Barbara having gone home to see her Savior, I am going to tell you a story that Barbara shared with me after insisting that I keep it to myself.

"Since Robert had been blessed to survive all his combat missions in WWII, Barbara would try to meet with the wives of aviators in the Korean conflict to provide encouragement and hope that their husbands would come home alive as Robert had. Barbara not only prayed with them but also promised to be there for them if their spouse did not return alive. She knew the prospect of widowhood was not talked about but was in the mind of each woman. Barbara ensured that they would not feel alone with this thought and that each woman had someone to be there so she would not feel alone.

"It seemed fitting for me to tell you this story today when I saw the wife of a decorated fighter pilot hugging Robert. I know Barbara would have greatly appreciated the favor being returned to her loving husband."

As the priest's words echoed through the quiet church, the weight of his message settled over the congregation. Quiet gasps and muffled sobs could be heard, while others sat in stunned silence, absorbing the story of Barbara's kindness. Robert, seated in the front row, clenched his hands tightly, his gaze fixed on the floor as memories of Barbara flooded his mind. She had been the heart of their family, and now, her absence felt like an immeasurable void.

After the funeral, Wade refused to attend church. Deeply affected by his mother's death, Wade stayed in his room for hours and then days. Wade had always been closer to his mom, while Rem and his dad had lived for ranching.

About a month after Barbara died, Wade began lifting weights as a way to deal with his anger and sadness. His fitness regime was so effective that he became a fanatic, never missing his workout routine. For the first time, he felt respect from his peers.

Their fitness routine paid off. When the boys entered high school, they became standouts in football, with scholarship offers from many colleges across the nation.

Wade had become a solid mass of muscle and was ranked as the #1 high school linebacker in the state of Colorado.

While Wade did poorly academically in school, Rem graduated with honors and was offered an academic scholarship to attend Princeton.

Robert had attended Yale, and he encouraged Rem to enroll at an Ivy League school. He wanted Rem to experience more of the world and to meet people from other parts of the United States before deciding what to do with his life. Robert knew that if Rem went to college in Colorado, he would have come home most weekends to help at the ranch.

Despite receiving numerous offers for athletic scholarships, Wade refused to attend college. Robert had hoped Wade would select Colorado University as his school of choice. The proximity would have allowed Robert to attend games on Saturdays and spend time with the professors who headed the aeronautics program. Instead, Wade chose to marry his high school sweetheart right after graduation, then move to the ranch near Sedalia. Married life, however, was not Wade's style; he was divorced one year later. From then on, there would be a long parade of women in Wade's life, the joke in Denver being that Wade had more women than he had horses.

On most weekends, Wade could be found drinking and dining in exclusive Denver bars and restaurants. Living such a lavish lifestyle quickly led to his ranch being severely neglected. On multiple occasions, Wade stayed away from the ranch for days. To mitigate Wade's carelessness, Rem had to drive over to feed and water the livestock. The horses in the corral would be kicking the empty galvanized water tanks, and the cattle would come running across the pasture when they heard Rem's pickup coming up the driveway loaded with bales of hay.

On one occasion while tending Wade's ranch, Rem found a horse tangled in a barbed wire fence. It appeared the horse had been suffering for days and had severed the flexor tendon in his left front leg. The damage was beyond repair. Knowing there was no time or reason to wait for the vet, Rem's heart was heavy, but he knew that he needed to end the horse's suffering. It wasn't the first time Rem had made the difficult decision, but knowing that the animal had been exhausted, trapped by his injuries, and left to die alone touched Rem. After he pulled the trigger, Rem stayed near the horse while it died.

Anger coursed through Rem as he thought of Wade's betrayal, his fists clenching at the memory. He wanted to confront Wade, demand answers, but his mother's dying words echoed in his mind, urging him to stay composed.

Round Top Mountain was north of Castle Rock. Local historians knew it as a spiritual meeting place for Native American tribes when they ruled the West.

Beyond its role in native lore, the top was a signal point, a lighthouse of sorts. Its location allowed smoke signals to be seen far and wide from Hilltop in Parker, Devil's Head in the foothills, and Wildcat Mountain directly west. On clear days, signals were visible from 25 miles in any direction.

Round Top was also a rallying point for Native Americans, who likely referred to it as "Truce Mountain." Since tribes were not always at peace with each other, it was deemed neutral territory by all. When meetings took place, the braves who came would lay their weapons down ritualistically before taking the summit. This made the mountain also useful as a point of departure for annual meetings held in Manitou Springs. Since the chieftains left on peaceful terms, the ride south allowed for useful discussions among tribes that had been warring with each other before.

CHAPTER 6
DESERTED

In middle age, Wade continued to drink and hang out with a crowd of high rollers in Denver. He was always short of money, but his friends were under the impression that he was rich because he incessantly reminded them that he owned three ranches in Douglas County.

After Robert died, Wade took full advantage of the power of attorney document that Robert had signed before his trip to Europe, Wade borrowed money by signing a mortgage on his ranch and the family's other two ranches. The ranches were owned by the Trust Robert had formed, and the power of attorney gave Wade the right to sign on behalf of the Trust.

In addition to borrowing against the three ranches, Wade also dipped heavily into the family's cash and stocks. Investing close to one million dollars, Wade bought a major share in a Nevada real estate venture with several of his high-roller friends and some famous athletes. Since the athletes were well-known, respected national figures,

Wade was confident that he was sitting on a gold mine. And even if the venture failed, Wade's power of attorney would protect him from any liability.

One day the family's attorney called Rem and informed him, "I just found out—and wanted to let you know immediately—that the real estate investment company in Nevada just declared bankruptcy."

Confused, Rem asked, "What real estate investment company? I have no idea what you're talking about."

With shock in his voice, the attorney said, "Wade didn't tell you he made this investment? He took out mortgages on all three ranches and sold the stocks in the family Trust. Except for your ranch, the other two ranches have already had foreclosure notices filed against them. Your ranch has a different bank handling the loan. The other two ranches were with the same bank. Rem, I am so sorry. Let me know if I can help in any way."

Stunned, Rem hung up the phone and walked down to the barn to clear his head. How could his brother have done something so foolish? Rem knew that he needed to get his ranch legally separated from the family Trust so that he could deal with the upcoming mortgage default. If Rem was unable to fix the mess Wade had created, he would lose everything. At almost 50 years old, it would not be easy for him to start over.

Rem had no idea how to tell his wife Jane what Wade had done. He was concerned about how Jane would respond to the news, since she had always had contempt for

Wade and had repeatedly asked Rem to leave the family Trust. He knew that she was right, but he had wanted to keep his dad's legacy alive since Robert was the one who had purchased all three ranches. Rem had also promised his mom that he would look out for Wade.

Neither Jane nor Rem knew the story Robert had told Wade about the death of Wade's father. If they had known the entire story, perhaps they would have understood why Rem's pleasant little brother had become so cynical and standoffish.

With Rem and Jane's two sons not living at home any longer, Jane was spending most of her time volunteering with the League of Women Voters or playing tennis. Born into a wealthy East Coast family, Jane had never enjoyed ranch life. And after 23 years of marriage, it had become quite evident that Jane didn't enjoy Rem any longer either. It wasn't long before she informed him that since they were not seeing eye-to-eye on most things, she planned to leave in two days to decompress at her parent's home in Connecticut and have time to think. Not long after her departure, she decided to file for divorce and not return to Douglas County.

Rem and Jane had met when he was at Princeton and she was at Sarah Lawrence. Jane had grown up in Connecticut, and she thoroughly enjoyed New York City and the Jersey shore. Despite their differences, it was love at first sight. They were married in her hometown of Bridgeport, Connecticut. The wedding was elegant, and the guests included many senators and congressmen. The New York City newspapers published a wedding write-up with photos on the society page.

At the wedding reception, Rem was proud of his rancher father. When the senator from Virginia (who was also the CEO of Pan Am) walked over to congratulate Rem on his marriage, the senator shook his hand and said, "Remington, all the best to the two of you. It's been great seeing your dad again. He seems so happy with his decision to be a rancher, but we miss him in DC. I'm sure you were aware that the president was considering him for a cabinet position when your father decided to go to Colorado."

Rem replied, "Senator, I had no idea that had happened, since I was quite young at the time. However, I do know how happy he has been, and I feel he made the right decision."

Thanking the senator for attending the wedding, Rem smiled as he added, "Let me tell you a story about my dad now that he is older. One day we were riding on horseback, rounding up cattle. As we took a break—with one leg over our saddle horns—he looked over at me and said, "Rem, recently I asked myself a very important question. If I could go back in time, would I do a single thing differently? My answer is that I don't think I would. Why? Because all the different roads I traveled and the choices I made have led me to where I am right now, shaping me into who I am. I am so grateful for what I have—even for what I don't have."

Rem smiled as he recalled his father's words to him, shaking his head as he continued, "My dad said, 'Son, life doesn't get any better than being able to say with full confidence that you have had the time of your life during your lifetime.'"

Even though Jane had agreed to move west with Rem to run the family's ranches, she had tried to convince him to stay on the East Coast after they were married. She proposed that they could spend part of every summer on the ranch and make trips to Colorado to ski during the holidays. They already had a place to live at the ranch, and she and her father owned a condo in Aspen. She was convinced she could change Rem's mind.

Hoping to move forward with her plan, she had preemptively spoken with her father about offering Rem a job at his stock brokerage firm in New York City. Seeing that Rem had graduated number one in his class from Princeton with a degree in finance, his future father-in-law knew that Rem was more than qualified for the role. Knowing many other companies were after Rem's services, Jane's father offered him a salary that would have impressed anyone—other than a cowboy, that is.

Looking back, Jane could vividly recall her dismay when Rem's response to her dad had been, "Thank you so much for the generous offer, but Jane and I are headed for Colorado to run my dad's ranches. My dad wanted me to have a good education so that I would be capable of bringing the ranches into the next century. Sir, I have been waiting four years to get back to where my heart is. Colorado is where I belong. Thank you again for your great offer, and I hope you understand why I can't accept it."

Although Jane was disappointed, she had agreed to move with Rem. Their plans were set in stone, just as their vows had bound their lives together.

The morning after the wedding, Rem woke up very early and silently made his way downstairs while everyone else was still asleep. He opened the French doors and slowly meandered out to the veranda overlooking the ocean. He needed to clear his head since they were leaving later that afternoon for their European honeymoon.

After speaking with Jane and her father, Rem realized that Jane was genuinely opposed to living on a horse ranch in Douglas County, Colorado. After all, she had gone out of her way to ask her father to give him a job somewhere far away from where he intended to build a life with Jane. They had somehow each convinced themselves that the other would change their mind. Would they truly be able to agree on a compromise, or would their differences grow into a recurring problem for their marriage?

As Rem stared at the ocean and listened to the waves crashing against the rocky shore, he thought about what his dad used to say to him.

"Rem, to experience happiness and achieve satisfaction, a person must go along with the way they are wired and not try to fit into a world where they are not comfortable. You need to find somewhere to be that speaks to you. If you are living in the wrong world, nothing will feel good. You need to truly know what is going on in your heart, as well as your life. Take the time to connect the dots and see what is really happening. For some reason, too many people ignore connecting the dots."

Rem knew that his heart—and his life—were on the ranch. He and Jane would go to Colorado as soon as they returned from their honeymoon. He hoped that Jane would adjust and find happiness on the ranch by his side.

CHAPTER 7
WHAT TO DO?

Rem's anger grew as he reflected on Wade's betrayal in bankrupting the Trust. After waking up in a sour mood over the ordeal, he hoped a ride on Cimarron might clear his head. He was slow to roll out of bed, taking time for a cup of coffee from his favorite mug before walking out to the barn.

Overwhelmed by his worries, Rem did not saddle up but instead threw the saddle over the nearest fencepost. He slipped the halter off Cimarron, slapped him on the left flank, and watched him race out to the pasture. Jumping into his pickup, Rem started the engine and hit the gas pedal, spinning the tires on the gravel. He needed time to think. Before departing through the ranch's main gate, he suddenly slammed on the brakes as he remembered to put the "Help Wanted" sign on the fence.

As Rem drove onto the main road, he remembered how his dad used to say to him, "Life isn't fair. Understand that you need to play the hand you were dealt. Live your life like it was a card game… it's all about the choices you make. "As Kenny Rogers' song goes, 'You need to know when to hold 'em, know when to fold 'em,' a lesson Rem's dad always lived by."

Driving had calmed his nerves, but soon it was time to return to the ranch to feed the horses. When he arrived, he saw a car parked in front of the barn and a woman walking up to the barn door. Curious, he parked his pick-up next to her car and approached the woman, noticing that she appeared to be around his age. As she turned to look at him, she smiled.

Rem's mouth went dry, making him feel like he was back in high school. Wide, questioning blue eyes met his gaze, a flicker of curiosity and hesitation in her expression. Rem found himself admiring her graceful confidence, her beauty enhanced by the way she carried herself—self-assured yet approachable.

In addition to being a football star in high school, Rem had been told that his female classmates found him extremely attractive. But despite his good looks and athletic ability, Rem was shy.

His dad's words echoed in his mind: "Rem, if you like her, don't keep it to yourself. You might be surprised—she might feel the same way."

"I guess you're right, Dad. Megan is different than the other girls. There's just something about her that I like. But what if she laughs at me or something?"

"Well, if she's anything like what you say, she's not going to laugh at you. You're a good-looking kid with a good head on *your shoulders. What's not to like?" Robert slapped Rem on the shoulder and said, "Now, let's get to work."*

For months, friends had been telling Rem about girls who were interested in him, but the news did not inspire any real confidence. One day, however, a girl who sat next to him in English class turned to him and said, "Rem, you need to ask Megan out. She is head over heels for you."

That's all it took. Megan was a petite cheerleader—only 5'2"—with long red hair, freckles, a warm smile, and a lively personality. Rem constantly found himself stealing glances at her when he thought she wasn't looking. He had become totally taken with her during the spring of their junior year but had been too shy to ask her out. Now, as a senior, he had made the decision to invite her to the Homecoming Dance.

On Monday morning, Rem walked slowly down the hall before the first bell rang. He took a deep breath as he approached her locker.

"Hi, Megan," he began nervously. "I wanted to see if you were available to go to the Homecoming Dance with me."

Looking up at him and smiling, Megan replied, "I really would love to, but Jim asked me last weekend and I said yes. I feel so bad because I'd love to go with you, Rem."

Glancing over her shoulder, she lowered her voice. "I probably shouldn't say this, but I have been hoping since last year that you would ask me out. How about the weekend after the dance? Would that be okay?"

Rem replied, "Count on it—I'll be looking forward to seeing you then."

✢✢✢

Rem scored three touchdowns in the Homecoming game. The dance to celebrate Homecoming directly followed the game, but Rem decided to drive home instead of going to the dance alone. He did not want to see Megan all dressed up and dancing with Jim. As he laid down that evening, he could only think about their date next Saturday and seeing her smile. He had gone on dates before, but never one where he liked the girl so much. His mind swirled with questions: Should he open her car door? Should he try to hold her hand? What would he wear? What would they do on their date? Eventually, Rem drifted off to sleep.

The next morning, his dad woke him early, saying, "I need you to come down to the barn." This is unusual, Rem thought. His dad usually let him sleep in the morning after his Friday night football games. As he dressed, he hoped that nothing had happened to Lily, his favorite quarter-horse mare. She was ready to go into labor any day.

When Rem entered the barn, he saw his dad sitting on a hay bale outside the tack room. He motioned for Rem to come over and sit next to him.

Looking somber, Robert began speaking. "Son, I would give anything not to have to tell you this. Coach called this morning. Last night, after the Homecoming dance, a carload of your friends were involved in a terrible accident. Five are in the hospital, but one died." He paused, then added, "Rem, It was Megan. I know you really liked her."

Stunned, Rem looked at his dad as tears streamed down his cheeks, murmuring, "Thanks for letting me know. If it's okay with you, I think I just want to saddle up and go for a ride."

Nodding, his father watched as Rem mounted his horse.

As Rem galloped across the valley, he kept thinking Why? Why do these things happen? Megan was gone and he would never see her again. If I had asked her to go to the Homecoming dance earlier, would she still be alive? Is her death my fault? He kept riding for the rest of the morning, praying that God would give him answers to his questions.

Rays of sunlight filtered through the trees as he rode along Plum Creek. The fall colors of the leaves resembled a painter's palette. To the west were majestic snow-capped peaks that included Longs Peak to the north and Pike's Peak to the south. Their beauty was eclipsed by Rem's sadness as he mourned the loss of Megan. He dismounted his horse, stumbled to the ground, and found himself sobbing uncontrollably.

Rolling onto his back in a bed of yellow and red leaves, he stared at the beautiful robin's-egg-blue Colorado sky and whispered to himself, "I wonder which cloud is taking Megan to heaven?"

Rem's feelings of guilt and loneliness continued to haunt him the rest of his senior year. The prospect of asking someone out on a date made his stomach twist. Worried, Robert watched his son struggle but was unable to help. Eventually, Robert realized that Rem needed to deal with his feelings on his own.

Going off to college brought some comfort to Rem; the change of scenery and friendships with classmates eased his heartache. Rem welcomed the challenges of college but knew that his sadness would never go away completely.

CHAPTER 8
TO BE FREE

Callie felt the soft breeze caress her face as she headed out for her morning jog. Ever since high school, she had jogged regularly to relax her nerves.

She cherished life in Douglas County, where the trails offered unmatched natural splendor. As she jogged through the towering Ponderosa pines, the scent of pine carried on the breeze invigorated her. She paused momentarily to take in the stunning view of the Front Range foothills and distant snow-capped peaks. This moment of peace deepened her connection to the landscape, reaffirming her love for her home with every visit.

As she turned the bend at the halfway point of her five-mile jog, she looked up at the beautiful blue sky, allowing her thoughts to take over. Taking in the sights of the mesas and rocky steep cliffs to the south, she wondered, *What can I do to make my life happier? I want to feel peace and contentment.*

After her jog, Callie showered and decided to take a drive to further clear her head. Driving along Highway 105, she noticed a majestic-looking horse galloping across a pasture to her left. Its mane and tail blew in the wind as the horse raced across the hillside. Callie admired this symbol of true freedom. The horse's muscles rippled under its glossy coat as it galloped, mane streaming like a banner in the wind. It moved with such effortless grace that Callie couldn't help but feel a pang of longing for that kind of freedom. A thought came to her suddenly: *Am I causing my own pain by allowing others to steal my freedom?*

Callie pulled over to the side of the road, feeling as if she had reached a turning point. As she sat in the car, the hum of passing traffic faded into the background. The warm leather of the seat pressed against her back as she let out a shaky breath, her fingers tightening around the steering wheel. For the first time, she felt the stirrings of hope that change was possible.

Callie had always liked the line, "Enjoy the journey; we are all just traveling through." Her DNA was telling her that now was the time to be happy and content. She had always felt that contentment—that feeling of being satisfied and not needing more—was the key. Once you had that, happiness was the result.

For her entire life, she had been a follower and had just wanted to be part of the crowd. She finally understood that change was needed.

Opening the car window, she felt the soft wind blowing in her hair as she uttered the words, "The only way to live life is to take some risks and not have any regrets." She smiled as she adopted her new mantra. Her favorite word since childhood had always been *fortuitous*—a word she defined as something that happened by lucky chance. She felt ready to take the necessary risks to find happiness.

Glancing across the road, Callie noticed a "Help Wanted" sign posted on the fence. She knew nothing about horses or ranching, she hesitated, thinking it might be better to simply write down the phone number and call later.

Then she remembered her vow to take risks. Realizing she had nothing to lose, she drove through the gate and parked near the barn. As she walked toward the door of the barn, she heard a pickup approach and park beside her car. Thinking it might be the owner, she decided to talk with him about the job.

As she waited by the barn door, she nervously wondered why she was there. It simply did not make any sense whatsoever. She did not need a part-time job to earn money. She knew nothing about chores on a ranch. Was it possible that today was one of those *fortuitous* moments?

Callie had no memory of when or how it started, but her favorite word, *fortuitous,* had always shaped her outlook on life. Instead of trying to control everything that happened, she felt that life required a decision here and there with a little bit of luck mixed in. Even though she did not seek fortuitous moments, she accepted them when they materialized.

She watched closely as a man stepped out of the pickup and walked towards her. His denim blue shirt with the sleeves rolled up, along with his Stetson hat, and large silver belt buckle made her feel like she was in a western movie. With twinkling dark brown eyes and wavy brown hair with glints of silver, he spoke in a low, gentle voice. "Hi, I'm Rem Cunningham… and you are…?"

Looking up at his six-foot-two-inch frame, Callie began talking so fast she wondered if she was suffering from heat stroke. Blushing under his steady gaze, she stuttered, "I'm Rose Callie Parker. Rose is also my grandmother's name. I have no idea why I just told you that."

She took a deep breath to collect herself and reached forward to shake his hand. "A pleasure to meet you, Rem. You can call me Callie. When I saw your Help Wanted sign, I decided to pull in. I know nothing about horses or ranching, but I'm a hard worker even though I don't need to earn money." Realizing she was rambling, she took a deep breath and blurted out, "Do you believe in fortuity?"

Amused, Rem smiled, shaking her hand as he spoke. "My full name is Remington. I was named after my grandfather, just as you were named after your grandmother. My grandfather was the only person who ever called me Remington. Now we are even."

Before responding to Callie's question, he thought carefully about what to say. "Callie, I believe in fortuity, but logic tells me that I should not hire a suburban lady like yourself to feed horses and muck stalls."

Then he looked at her and added, "Rose Callie Parker, if I say yes to hiring you, how many hours would you be available to work every week?"

Surprised, she cleared her throat to suppress her nerves and replied confidently, "I could work four hours a day, around two or three days each week."

To his astonishment, Rem nodded and smiled. "Can you start tomorrow?"

With a radiant smile, Callie nodded.

Grinning, Rem turned towards his pickup, then looked at Callie and said, "I'll see you at 8 a.m. sharp—be sure to bring leather gloves and wear boots."

Before going to bed that evening, Callie made an entry in her journal.

May 13, 1999

Dear Journal,

Bill is out of town again, so what. I think I'm lonelier when he's here than when he's gone. Anyway, I have the entire evening to myself. I'm feeling restless, so I think a glass of red wine while curled up in my favorite chair will be the perfect way to spend my evening.

Corny as it sounds, I feel like today was the first day of the rest of my life. So many things have been weighing heavily on my mind. The future has no guarantees. What makes one thing happen and not another? What causes someone to flourish or die, or take another course? Wow—these questions seem so deep to contemplate, but I often feel that life dictates the directions we take.

While driving today, I saw a stallion galloping in the wind and envied his freedom. Then I noticed a Help Wanted sign on a fence post. I thought, "How fortuitous" (I know, my favorite word), so I drove in. It was at that very moment that I met a man who took my breath away. I was instantly drawn in by his gentle brown eyes. The energy between us was undeniable. Even his name sounded strong and sexy....... Remington Cunningham. At that very moment, I felt my life leading me in a new direction. My heart felt lighter, as if a weight was lifting.

I actually applied for a ranch-hand position. Can you believe it? Imagine my surprise when he said he would hire me and asked if I could start tomorrow! All of this is so crazy—I haven't allowed myself to think like this in years (if ever!). I am feeling so alive, as if something has awakened inside of me. It makes my whole body tingle, and I love it!

Seriously, though, who is this new me I met today? I so want to reconnect with myself and discover WHO I AM again. I don't know what that looks like, but I want to let the real me come out and play! I feel like I'm beginning a journey of self-discovery, and it's so exciting.

For so long, I have been burying my feelings and ignoring hurts from my past. Letting go is an important part of moving forward, and I have made the decision to do that. I have to be honest with myself and admit what no longer works for me. I want to experience being alive. I want to feel again.

CHAPTER 9
THE MEADOWLARK WAS SINGING

The next morning Callie arrived at the ranch wearing blue jeans, with a new pair of leather gloves tucked in her back pocket. To her relief, she had found an old pair of western boots in her closet. She would have felt like a city slicker if she'd arrived for her first day wearing a brand-new pair of boots.

As she parked her car near the barn, she remembered how Rem had looked the day before. His wide shoulders and narrow hips were memorable, but the look in his smoldering brown eyes had made the deepest impression. It was as if they were speaking to her, extending an invitation.

Shaking her head, she attempted to clear her thoughts. It wasn't like her to react this way. At the same time, she remembered the galloping horse and her new mantra: *The only way to live life is to take some risks with no regrets.*

Callie had often wondered if her past misfortunes had not only diminished her interest in men but also eroded her ability to feel truly desired. Years of disappointment had left her cautious, yet seeing Rem reignited something she thought she had lost—a flicker of hope.

When Rem met her at the barn door, Callie's pulse quickened. His rugged appearance—biceps sculpted from years of ranch work and a confident yet unassuming smile—made her feel like a giddy teenager. She fought to steady her breath, wondering how this man could awaken feelings she thought had long faded.

They smiled at each other, and without saying a word, Rem passed her a hay fork and a pushcart. As they walked into the barn together, he showed her where the horse stalls were. The stalls were empty because the horses had been turned out to pasture for the day.

As they entered the first stall, Rem smiled slightly as he demonstrated how to pick up a clump of manure without taking too much straw along with it. Awkward at first, Callie soon got the hang of it and proceeded to fill the cart. When he was confident that she could proceed on her own, Rem instructed her to clean the stall and take the manure out to the back of the barn. Then he turned to leave, explaining, "I need to go train a young colt to accept being saddled for the first time. I'll be back later."

As she worked alone in the barn, Callie savored the aroma of alfalfa hay mixed with horses and leather. As she worked, the solitude brought a sense of calm that Callie had been longing for.

This situation reminded her of how a friend had explained the three W's required for true happiness: enjoying <u>W</u>ho you are with, liking <u>W</u>hat you are doing, and being <u>W</u>here you want to be. With a smile, Callie took a deep breath and continued to work.

As she pushed the cart down the concrete alleyway and out to the back of the barn, she heard a meadowlark celebrating the beautiful summer morning. It had been years since she had paid attention to the song of the meadowlark.

When Callie was a little girl visiting her grandmother Rose, she used to listen to the meadowlarks as her grandmother tended her rose garden. Grandma told her, "Callie, when I am sad or nervous, I come out here and let the song of the meadowlark lift my spirits. The meadowlark welcomes you at the start of the day and bids you farewell as the sun sets."

Intrigued, Callie listened closely as her grandmother shared more information.

"Meadowlarks have a complex, two-phase primary song that begins with one to six whistles and descends to a series of one to five gurgling warbles."

Oh, how she missed Grandma Rose! Callie had never felt more secure than she had when she was curled up in Grandma's lap, listening to stories about what it had been like to grow up in Germany. Callie's favorite story was of her grandmother leaving Bremerhaven, Germany, on a steamer ship bound for New York City. Crossing the ocean with her family and enduring storms along the way seemed like a daring feat for a little eight-year-old girl. Grandma Rose was—and always would be—her hero.

Callie felt comfortable and at peace in Rem's barn. For the first time in decades, she had a sense of contentment. She had known for some time that her current life no longer resembled what she had wanted it to be. She could visualize how it would feel to be closer to her true self.

***

As Callie's days on the ranch turned into weeks, Callie and Rem continued to work well together. Rem looked forward to her arrival each day and felt like something was missing on the days when she was absent. Somehow, although he couldn't put his finger on how she did it, Callie made each day a little more special.

Rem had noticed that Callie was quieter than most of the women he had encountered. It wasn't that she didn't like to talk; rather, she only talked when she had something to say. Perhaps her contemplative nature instilled meaning in every word she spoke. At times, her thoughts seemed distant, drifting elsewhere as she mechanically carried out her chores.

Occasionally he would look over and notice that she was smiling for no apparent reason. It always made him wonder what she was thinking about.

When they did get a chance to talk, Rem was impressed with how astute Callie was. He discovered that she had graduated from college with honors, but academics aside, he was most impressed by her kind spirit. She never judged anyone or anything but simply accepted people for who they were instead of what she wanted them to be.

While Rem had been getting to know Callie, she had also been learning about him. During some of their conversations she sensed that he was deeply troubled. Not wanting to ask questions that might seem intrusive, she struggled to find the best way to broach the subject. She knew very little about the issues involving Rem's brother and the potential impact on the ranch's future, but she wanted to ask because she genuinely cared. Actually, she cared more than she wanted to admit.

Rem loved talking with Callie. Their shared conversations flowed easily, and he never needed to worry about choosing the right words. He knew he could say anything without fear of being seen in a negative light.

One day after they'd finished their chores earlier than usual, Rem surprised Callie by saying, "Would you like to have a beer?" Smiling, Callie nodded, surprised by her own eagerness.

"I'm a Chardonnay girl, but a beer actually sounds wonderful," she agreed.

Rem took a six-pack from the refrigerator and they sat down at a picnic table under a grove of cottonwood trees.

After relaxing and enjoying some good laughs, Rem turned to Callie. His face became serious as he blurted out, "Callie, I am in deep financial trouble. I need to talk with someone I can trust…someone who cares." Touched by his willingness to be vulnerable, she waited for him to continue.

"My attorney and CPA say they care, but I don't think they really do. To them, I'm just another client with a problem. My bank is calling my loan."

His normally strong voice quavered as he added, "If I don't agree to the new loan they have proposed, they're threatening to foreclose on the ranch and file liens on all my equipment and automobiles. Tomorrow I am expected to appear in bankruptcy court regarding my brother emptying out the family Trust of money and mortgaging the ranches."

Although she felt stunned by Rem's news, Callie was determined not to show it. She tried to look supportive as he continued.

"My attorney and I will be appearing to see if we can remove my ranch from the umbrella of the Trust. My hope is that the loan officer will appear and plead that their loan security is on my ranch alone, whereas the other two ranches are under a Trust umbrella loan. If he wins, they will have the right to be in the first loan position on my ranch and not part of the bankruptcy. At least that's what I'm hoping for. If I can get my ranch separated from the bankruptcy and my brother, I can take on the bank and win."

With a sigh, Rem leaned against a big cottonwood tree. He contemplated telling her about his marital situation but decided that the topic was too personal of a topic to bring up after what he had just shared with her. All Callie knew was that Rem was married and for some reason his wife was spending the summer in Connecticut.

"Rem, of course you can trust me, and I do care." Reaching out to place her hand gently on his shoulder, Callie felt compassion beyond anything she had felt before. "I am always be available to listen, but I'm afraid I will be short on advice. Just know that whatever happens, Rem, I truly believe in you. Look at everything you have accomplished. I know that you have what it takes to overcome this challenge. I believe this, so you need to believe it too!"

Turning to Callie, Rem looked at her and spoke softly as their eyes met. "You truly are my angel. Your support means more to me than I can say. Thank you so much."

June 2, 1999

Dear Journal,

Rem opened up a bit more today about what is going on in his life. The things that are troubling him. Everyone—no matter how strong they are—needs to feel understood, without fear of judgment when they are stressed and scared. Rem is no exception. I wanted to be there for him today. I think he needed a woman's touch—someone who would be comforting, even tender.

Although Rem did open up about his business troubles, he has yet to say anything about his wife. I thought he might mention her today—not that he has to—but I must admit I have wondered what the real story is about her.

It always amazes me at how easily our conversations flow. It never feels strained between us. I love that he feels so comfortable with me and that we have a trust that allows us to talk so openly with each other. There is such a tenderness about him—in his eyes, his voice, his actions. It isn't often that you meet such a strong yet truly gentle man. When he called me "his angel" today, I honestly felt like I was going to melt! What a compliment!

I thought that men like him didn't exist. As little girls, we dream about them but it seems the hard realities of life tell us otherwise. Now, too late, I find out that they do.

CHAPTER 10
THE BARN WAS DARK

The next morning, as Callie was currying a large bay horse, she heard Rem's boots as he walked down the concrete alleyway between the stalls. She could see his image without even turning, feeling a flutter in her heart. The rhythmic sound of hay hitting the stalls filled the barn as she imagined him lifting heavy bales from the wagon. His straining biceps and strong, compact frame made her pulse quicken as he bent to cut the twine. She knew he would be covered in sweat, which would make him glisten like a Greek god.

She whispered to herself, "Oh, Callie, quit thinking like that. You are way too old, and you're a married woman." Her knees felt a little weak as she tried to get some distance from her attraction to Rem.

Even though she considered herself a city girl, she had grown to love the horse barn. Its rustic beauty spoke of history and a forgotten way of life. A time when hard work was the foundation for success. A time when romance could be found in the simplest of places.

When she finished currying the bay horse, she walked him to his stall and removed his halter and lead rope. Then she headed to the next stall to get a paint horse named Cochise. She adored this little mare who was due to foal any day now. As she guided Cochise down the concrete alleyway, she looked over and saw Rem talking on his cell phone. Irritation was evident in his tone of voice.

After the phone conversation ended, Rem marched out of the barn with his hat in hand. Her curiosity about his terse tone on the phone lingered as she watched him saddle Cimarron with determined precision. What could have made him so upset? She wanted to ask but feared crossing an invisible boundary.

Even watching him ride riveted Callie's attention. With his legs wrapped around Cimarron, he rode in sync with the motion of the horse. So beautiful, so free.

Returning about an hour later, Rem tied Cimarron in the center of the alleyway with lead ropes extending from each side. Removing Cimarron's bridle, he clipped the lead ropes to the halter. As he reached down to remove the girth strap on the saddle, Callie approached him and said, "Can I curry and brush him down or would you like me to give him a bath? He looks sweaty from that hard ride." As she spoke, she reached out tentatively, her fingers brushing the soft leather of the halter, trying to steady her nerves.

Looking at her, he said softly, "No, Callie, I will do it, but thanks for asking. I'm sorry for taking off, but that was my wife calling from Connecticut. I don't think she is coming back. But here is the crazy thing that I'm all mixed up about. I didn't really want her to return home."

"Rem...I..." she said, stopping herself mid-sentence. Rem's somber expression told her that now was not the time to say anything else. Before stepping away, Callie looked up at Rem and said, "I'll give you some space to think. Let me know if you need anything."

Nerves on edge, Callie resumed currying the little paint mare. Rem's words had surprised her, and she wondered if she was reading too much into them. She reminded herself that she was married to Bill, and Rem was also married. She could have all the sexy daydreams she wanted, but that was as far as it would go. Callie was a devoted mother to her boys and a loving daughter to her parents. Even though her relationship with Bill was unfulfilling, she *was* still married to him.

Rem began to curry and brush Cimarron, but as Callie walked away, his gaze followed her. He had been studying her lips for weeks. So luscious and inviting. He thought about his lips parting hers with the pressure from a long and sensual kiss. Then he thought about the shapely breasts under her tight-fitting cotton work shirt. Watching her bend over to clean stalls was beyond sexy.

Rem was aware that his admiration for Callie went beyond her physical attractiveness. She had an aura and mystic beauty that fascinated him. He was attracted to her both physically and emotionally... by the way she moved and talked...by the look in her eyes. Callie was everything he had been searching for and more.

On an impulse, he walked up the concrete alley towards her. When he was right behind her, he touched her shoulder and gently swung her around. Without warning, he leaned forward and kissed her.

Too stunned for words, Callie pushed him away and ran out of the barn. He watched as she got into her car and drove away.

Realizing the gravity of his mistake, he was certain that the odds of seeing her again were slim. Why had he done that? It had been much too soon to make such a bold move. The urge to touch her had overcome him.

Rem spent the rest of the afternoon doing ranch chores in a daze. He thought about the impending divorce from Jane and what that would entail. It would be emotionally taxing for him and the boys. He wondered what Jane was going to ask for in the divorce papers. Fortunately, she had a wealthy family and a substantial trust fund. Her assets would help in any court proceedings.

His mind turned back to Callie. Was it possible that he would never see her again? He would not be able to come to terms with that. They were connected in a way that he had never experienced before. In his gut, he knew that Callie also felt the magic.

Maybe he would see her again. If so, he sure as hell would not make another move on her. He just needed her nearby. Being around her made him feel so alive. The world felt right when he could see her in the barn or chat with her under the cottonwood trees.

June 3, 1999

Dear Journal,

I think I made a mistake today. Or maybe I didn't. I don't know what to think. He kissed me. His lips felt amazing. I've imagined this moment in my head so many times, but I got scared. I ran. I feel like I could fall too fast for him, like I could get lost in him. I can't let myself do that. Yet, I long so much to be close to him, to feel him. To feel him in a way that a woman wants to feel a man. He awakens something in me that I didn't know was there. He makes me feel so alive.

I remember an older person telling me once, "You will have more regrets about the things in life that you did not do than the things you did do."

It all seems so fortuitous. My newfound curiosity and thirst for adventure tells me to just let it play out and not try to control everything.

It reminds me of the famous old line, "Life is either a daring adventure or nothing at all." But I am not sure how to handle this. It's not fair of me to play mind games with Rem. I at least owe him a straightforward explanation as to why I ran. I need to apologize and let him know that I got scared because of the feelings I've been having for him.

How can I quit the job when that means I will never see him again? I treasure every moment we have had together. We are always so lighthearted, happy and laughing all the time. Every day I catch him stealing glances my way, and I can't help smiling to myself. The brush of our hands or arms when we work closely together always gives me butterflies. The anticipation of what could be next is exhilarating.

I feel a trust in Rem that I've never experienced before. I never thought I would trust a man again and show my vulnerable side. When was the last time I was able to feel more than surface level? To be able to share all my thoughts and dreams, achievements and strengths, insecurities and weaknesses without the fear of being judged. Or, for my words to just fall on deaf ears. What would it feel like to have true, uninhibited intimacy?

CHAPTER 11
WHO MADE THE MISTAKE?

Much to Rem's surprise, Callie arrived at the ranch the next morning as usual. Without saying a word, they acknowledged each other with a nod and started doing their chores.

Callie could barely keep her thoughts in line as she recounted the previous day's events. She was lost in contemplation, her heart pounding nervously as she picked up a broom from the tack closet and swept away the dust on the barn floor. Should she say something? Should she let it go? She was a married woman, and Rem's kiss yesterday should have made her furious, yet there was something special about Rem that made it feel so right.

After about an hour of near silence, Rem could no longer avoid talking to Callie. After thinking about what he'd done the previous day, he knew it would be better to say something than to avoid the topic altogether. He approached her cautiously in the breezeway.

After taking a deep breath, he said, "Callie, please accept my apology for what I did yesterday. I have no idea what came over me, but I know that's not a good excuse. However, I must mention that I enjoy the moments we share together. I find you so special. Saying all of that, I just don't know what to do with my feelings." Rem swallowed thickly, his mind racing as he wondered how Callie was going to react.

She looked up at him, her eyes sparkling and a tender smile playing upon her lips.

Taking a step toward him, she leaned forward, grasped his shoulders and closed her eyes as she tenderly pressed her lips to his. Her heart fluttered as she drew away slightly, whispering against his lips, "Don't apologize. I was the one who made a mistake yesterday."

Stunned, Rem stood before her with his heart beating wildly in his chest. He slowly stepped forward and drew her closer, guiding her torso to rest against his own. He gathered her in his arms and gently caressed her chin between his index finger and thumb, lifting her chin upward as he gazed into her eyes.

She tilted her head to the side and softly said, "Your eyes are looking into my soul. You have my permission to look deeply, but promise me that you will never take advantage of what you see."

He nodded, taking his time as he closed the gap between his mouth and hers. He pressed his lips to hers. His tongue explored her mouth as hers explored his. With all he had been going through, this moment was something his heart would never forget. Joy filled him as he heard the soft sounds Callie made as he touched her. Coming from deep in her throat and chest, they filled him with desire beyond anything he'd felt before.

Callie's body ached with an unfulfilled need; she grew dizzy and the air swirled around her taking control of her balance. As much as she truly desired him, she was afraid to go further.

Without saying a word, Rem lifted her off her feet and carried her into one of the stalls where she had just laid out fresh straw. Lying down beside her, he could hear her rapid breathing and see her chest heaving. It was a moment of intimacy that startled him but at the same time felt so natural. She circled her arms around his shoulders and embraced him tightly.

Rem could feel Callie's heart thudding against his chest. The warmth radiating from her body and the movement of her hips increased his excitement even more. She raised her head from his shoulder and gently placed her lips against his. They kissed slowly, tenderly at first, then deeply with abandonment. He knew what he wanted to do but knew it was not what she was searching for. He could see the tears welling up in her eyes, and he paused, wondering for a moment what she might be thinking.

Even with the fire raging in his loins, he knew now was not the time to take her for his own satisfaction.

With her hands caressing the back of his neck, she softly murmured, "In all the years I have been an adult—a woman—I have never experienced a feeling like this. I have read and dreamed about being swept off my feet, but have never experienced it for myself. I'm not sure if a lady is supposed to say thank you after a man has made her feel this way, but let me say thank you, Rem! Please know how much I appreciate your caring for me by not going further. I don't know if I could handle it at this time."

A few hours later, Rem watched Callie drive through the ranch gate and waved goodbye to her as he leaned up against the barn door. His eyes followed her car until it disappeared as she headed north on the highway. As he walked back toward the horse stalls, he stopped and looked into the stall in which he and Callie had almost made love. His mind started to race as fast as his heart.

He thought, *Never in my life have had feelings for a woman as I do for Callie. I've read about it in novels, seen it in movies, but I had always thought those scenes were embellished and never happened in real life. I'm so pleased, as difficult as it was, that I stopped. She is so confused and, like me, she doesn't know what to do about these feelings. To hurt her would tear me apart.*

June 4, 1999

Dear Journal,

I just sat down with my third glass of wine this evening. Life has tipped upside down for me and I'm feeling rather frisky tonight, perhaps even a little naughty. I keep playing the events from today over and over again in my head. I need intimacy. I can hardly stand it.

The moment his lips touched mine today, I felt everything within me change. His lips were so soft, so warm, so inviting. I loved the taste of him, the scent of him. He surprised me when he picked me up and carried me into the horse stall. My mind was spinning when I sank into the straw. I remember thinking, what am I doing?

But all thoughts left me as he began trailing kisses down my neck. His hardworking ranch hands were rough, but his tenderness showed in the way he touched me. I couldn't quit shaking. I felt as if it was a cry for all the things I had been looking for my entire life.

His touch was so soft, so gentle, so patient. He is unlike any other man I've ever been with. Why were other men so impatient and rough? Never in my life did I imagine that I would find a man who would understand how a woman needs to be touched.

CHAPTER 12
SPRING BECAME SUMMER

Rem was able to legally separate himself from the Trust's bankruptcy court proceedings. Even so, he still had to negotiate with the bank that held the mortgage on his ranch.

The negotiations centered on Rem not accepting the bank's terms that Wade had negotiated and agreed to. Rem wanted to take out a new loan instead of assuming Wade's loan, which had onerous terms and conditions. Now that Rem wasn't a party to the Trust's bankruptcy, the bank was willing to negotiate new loan terms with him.

He knew the bank had all the power and leverage to dictate the terms of the loan, but he felt that they were not quite as smart or cunning as he was. As is typical with banks, they had not done their research on the history of the borrower. If they had done so, they would have discovered he had a Bachelor of Science degree in Finance from Princeton University.

To ensure he had their full attention, he told them that another bank was interested in doing the new loan on the ranch. He explained that he had told them he would get back to them with his answer to the bank's most recent loan proposal.

Rem had heard that this Castle Rock bank had a reputation for being very competitive with other banks. They would not like being aced out and losing a potential customer. Rem knew he had to find a lender who would offer him a new loan commitment letter with better terms and conditions.

Rem called Ted, one of his college roommates who had become a banker in New York City. Rem asked Ted if he would put together a loan commitment letter for a new loan on his ranch. Rem went on to tell Ted the whole story of what had happened.

Ted was upset to hear what Rem was going through and was quick to recall that he owed Rem a big payback. Ted said he would prepare a loan commitment letter as a favor to Rem.

Ted explained to Rem that he wished that he could do the loan, but his bank did not want any loans in Colorado. The commitment letter would only be for the purpose of getting the attention of the Colorado bank. Ted's commitment letter offered a loan with an interest rate that was 1% lower than the Colorado bank's rate and a longer amortization term without a balloon payment involved.

After receiving the commitment letter from Ted via e-mail, Rem drove to the bank in Castle Rock to submit the letter to his loan officer. The loan officer told Rem that he would review the commitment letter and then take it to the loan committee to see if they could match the loan proposal from Ted's bank.

With his nerves frayed from the loan negotiations, Rem headed back to the ranch to see if Callie was still working. He needed to hear her calming voice and bask in her radiant smile. She had the face of an angel, and her attention never failed to lift his spirits.

As he drove through the main gate to the ranch, he was glad to see that her car was still parked in front of the barn. A smile spread across his face, and the tight muscles in his shoulders relaxed a bit. He parked his pickup next to Callie's car and opened the door to get out. He could not wait to look into her eyes and feel the serenity she brought.

"Rem, I didn't expect you to be back so soon. How did it go at the bank?"

"Callie, it went very well, and I think the bank is going to agree to my proposed loan terms. I'm so happy you're here. It feels so much better to share good news with you. I sure did not want to face turning on the lights in the barn without you here, Callie. I know you'll be late getting home and must run, but would it be okay if I gave you a big hug and a kiss?"

She ran to him and jumped into his arms, wrapping her legs around his body. Her lips sealed to his, with a deep, warm kiss that lingered. With a soft smile, she said, "You never have to ask, Cowboy. You have rounded me up and branded me. My heart is yours. I have to go now, but I will see you in the morning."

CHAPTER 13
AN UNFORGETTABLE RIDE

For several weeks, Callie had been hinting that she wanted to learn how to ride a horse. When she arrived at the ranch on Monday morning, Rem informed her that he would teach her to ride that day. He had already saddled an older, gentle gelding sorrel horse named Chief for her to feel safe on.

He took her hand and led her to Chief and said, "Callie, we always mount a horse from the left side. Put your left foot in the stirrup and with both hands grab the saddle horn. Now, pull yourself up and swing your right leg over the saddle."

Looking down from the saddle, Callie's eyes met Rem's. Smiling broadly, she said, "This feels really good, and I'm not nervous at all! I feel a sense of freedom in my body."

Rem smiled, watching Callie with care as he mounted Cimarron. As they left the gate, she stared at him from behind and with a laugh said, "Hey, Cowboy, you not only look good from the front side, but also from the back side."

Rem turned in his saddle and said, "Well, Ms. Parker, you need to pay attention to riding. If you don't, I'm going to put you up in my saddle with me and show you how much fun it is to trot with two people in one saddle."

Without hesitation Callie shouted back, "Mr. Cunningham, you are such a tease. Now let me tease you. Should I sit facing you, or is that too much fun for one ride?"

Rem shook his head and laughed, saying, "Callie, you never cease to amaze me. I'm not sure I'd fit right in the saddle with a third leg. You'd better ride facing front, just to keep me sane."

He decided to take the trail down to Plum Creek to show her the colossal cottonwood trees and the lush grass growing along the creek bed.

"Callie, I have ridden this same trail since I was eight years old, and I swear each time it just gets more beautiful. While we ride, I want you to take your time and look at everything around you, from the snow-capped mountains down to the colors of the beautiful grasses. I hope the feeling you get in your heart and soul while high above the ground on this beautiful beast will overwhelm you I want you to feel fully relaxed and on top of the world. The worries of the real world will take a back seat to that sense of inner peace."

Callie replied, "I'm already there, and I can't thank you enough for taking me riding and showing me this beautiful valley. I was never around horses when I was younger. I really love the smell of them and being part of their movements. I am hooked, and I would be more than happy to ride with you anytime you want."

Callie smiled, patting Chief on the neck as she took in the scenery around them. She glanced over to Rem, clearing her throat as she pointed ahead, "Rem, look over where the creek makes a bend. That beautiful grove of cottonwoods with the aspens mixed in is one of the most relaxing and serene sites I have ever seen. Can we go over there?"

Rem followed the direction Callie was pointing with his eyes, grimacing when he saw where she was pointing. He rolled his shoulders back as he thought for a moment, knowing that this would be an excellent opportunity to tell Callie a little more about his life before they met.

"Callie, I was not planning to take you over there today, but I feel I must since you asked. To be honest, I have avoided that grove since I was seventeen years old. When we get over there, I have a story to tell you. The story is about something that happened years ago."

They road silently through the hayfield toward the grove. Rem seemed pensive and thoughtful about what he had to tell Callie. When they reached the grove, Rem helped her dismount from Chief and took her hand to lead her to the tall grass where he had mourned Megan's death years ago. It felt like time had stood still. The leaves were gently blowing in the wind, creating a musical background like the sound of an orchestra with a row of violins softly moving their bows across the strings. Since it was only mid-morning, two morning doves were cooing their haunting song high in the trees.

"Callie, when I was a senior in high school, I had my first crush on a girl named Megan Flannigan. I asked her to the homecoming dance, but she already had a date. Years later I found out that she had gone out drinking with her girlfriends after the dance. That night, she was killed in an automobile accident. I blamed myself for months for not asking her out earlier. It was not until the following Spring that I learned the truth, which freed me from the guilt I was feeling."

A wave of sadness hit Rem as he continued talking. "The morning my dad told me that Megan had died, I saddled up and rode down to this grove to cry and pray for Megan. I remember lying on my back in this same spot for hours and looking up at the clouds, thinking Megan was riding on one of them. I haven't been here since."

With tears in her eyes, Callie wrapped her arms around him.

"Rem, you are so sensitive and such a good man. We can never understand why terrible things happen to good people. It is up to us to decide how to handle tragedy. Even though you never forgot Megan, you have led a good life."

Rem asked, "Callie, would you lay here with me and look up at the clouds? It's been a long time. I know you're not mine, Callie, so I probably shouldn't even say this. I don't think I could make it if anything happened to you. Or maybe I should say it this way: I would not want to go on living if there wasn't a Callie in my life."

In response, Callie rolled up on her elbows and gazed into his eyes as the sun peeked through the leaves. The doves seemed to coo in rhythm with her breathing. She thought, *Oh, how much I wish that I was only his.*

Rem helped Callie to her feet where they stood for a moment, listening to the rustling of the grasses, and the buzzing of nature. At the edge of the clearing, a wild rose bush in full bloom caught Callie's eye. Surely this was a sign that she was where she was meant to be, with the man she was meant to be with.

Before they mounted the horses, Callie walked to the rose bush and broke off one of the stems. She intended to keep the rose in the barn as a reminder of this day with Rem.

As they rode back to the ranch, Callie looked at Rem somberly as she explained, "Rem, I'm going to be gone for two weeks. My son is graduating as a Second Lieutenant from the Army Officers' School at Ft. Benning, Georgia. We're going to the graduation. The whole family—Bill too—I mean we're all going as a family. My sister in Savannah has invited us to spend our Fourth of July vacation at her house in Hilton Head after graduation."

"Callie, congratulations on Ben's graduation—Wow! A commissioned officer. You must be very proud. Don't worry, I won't fire you and I won't look for a new hand to take your place while you are gone, as long as you promise me one thing."

With a twist of her head and rapidly blinking eyes, she looked at Rem and asked, "What do I have to promise, Mr. Cunningham?"

"Well, Callie, you need to promise me that every day you will take a moment to listen to the meadowlarks singing and to imagine my lips on yours."

June 28, 1999

Dear Journal,

Rem took me riding down by Plum Creek this morning. I was so relaxed and felt oddly comfortable being on a horse for the first time. Rem so patient, and just being with him is a feeling I can't quite describe. He makes me feel so confident in myself, like I can do anything I set my mind to do. It was so serene with the prairie grasses blowing in the breeze. I swear the wind was whispering songs to us through the pines as we rode. I suppose that was all in my imagination, but it felt quite magical.

I asked him if we could stop and take a break in the beautiful grove of trees next to Plum Creek. Little did I know that the spot held a lot of sad memories for him. After he helped me off my horse, we sat under one of the large cottonwood trees. He told me about his first crush Megan's tragic accident and the emotional struggles he went through. I could feel his pain as he told me his story, but I could tell that he now had a sense of peace and acceptance. Surrounded by the trees in the beautiful summer sun, I held his hand as we sat talking about her.

After we had talked for quite some time, Rem laid me back on the cool morning grass. I became so turned on that I pushed him on his back and just stared into his eyes, knowing that I wanted him so badly. Even though

I could not go further, we explored and played and teased until we melted into each other.

I wanted to shout out, "Please take me… possess me." I felt a tear going down my cheek. Why the tear? Because I was so happy, yet overcome with sadness at the same time.

I have finally found everything I have ever wanted… a feeling of peace and freedom, the man I have dreamed about since I was a young girl, and a man who loves me.

However, I don't approve of what I am doing. It goes against everything I believe in and what my mom taught me.

Oh my God, to feel so happy yet so sad at the same time is more than I can handle.

I have only one lifetime, so do I live it the way I want or sacrifice it to follow the rules I have grown up to believe in and respect?

CHAPTER 14
MAGICAL CABIN

Rem stood with his hand wrapped around his coffee mug, thinking about Callie. He missed her. She lit up the ranch and made the days brighter. He stared out the kitchen window imagining her soft lips and the scent of her. Suddenly, his cell phone rang snapping him back to reality. He didn't recognize the number, but he answered it anyway with his usual greeting: "This is Rem Cunningham."

"Rem, this is Callie! I'm at a pay phone in the Savannah airport. I can't talk long, but I wanted to let you know that Bill left right after the graduation. He can't stand my sister. He went straight to LA from the ceremony. Now he texts me to tell me he's flying to Australia tomorrow for a medical seminar. I'm going to be home later today, and since he will be on an international flight for hours and hours, I can come see you and won't have to explain where I'm at. Does that sound like something you can handle, Cowboy?"

Laughing, he said, "I have two welcome home presents for you. I wish I could say more, but I know you can't talk long." Rem knew that Callie would be overcome with curiosity.

Knowing Callie had the whole evening free, he considered some plans. While looking at a picture of his mother on the wall, an idea struck him. He decided to take Callie to Evergreen to visit the cabin where his mother's parents had lived after retiring to Colorado, close to their only daughter, Barbara.

Grandpa had been a carpenter, and Grandma collected antiques. As a result, the inside of the cabin was more beautiful than any movie set he had ever seen. The decor was Rocky Mountain rustic, and he knew Callie would love it.

***

When Callie arrived at the ranch the next morning, they greeted each other as if they had been apart for two years instead of two weeks. She jumped up and put her arms around his neck, and Rem gave her a long, hard kiss and said, "I am going to take you somewhere today that I haven't been to for many years. As a matter of fact, I've never taken anyone else there. There is a very special cabin located a mile or so outside of Evergreen that my mother treasured almost more than anything else. I think the cabin kept her memories of her parents alive. After my mom's death, we discovered a handwritten codicil to her will requesting that the family never sell the cabin. She asked us to hire a local couple to maintain and clean it. My dad, of course, followed through with Mom's wishes, and after his death, Wade and I agreed to do the same.

"I rarely have time to visit the cabin, and my boys have no interest in it, so it is vacant almost all of the time. Callie, it is so quaint inside that it always makes me think of my grandma baking cookies in the kitchen. At the same time, it has a western mountain man flair that makes me think of my grandpa. He and I would sit by the fire with a big bowl of popcorn as he told me story after story about events in his life. Grandma used to shake her head whenever she knew he was exaggerating."

Rem decided to turn off the C-470 interstate at the Morrison Road exit. Highway 74 to Evergreen is picturesque, with steep canyon walls and Bear Creek flowing towards Denver.

Rem looked over at Callie and said, "Why don't we stop in Evergreen before going to the cabin? I know a place that makes the best double cheeseburger…and a great Greek salad for you."

After lunch, Rem drove to the cabin. As soon as he parked the pickup truck, Callie got out and ran up to the front door. She immediately noticed that the front porch was lined with wild rosebushes. Callie turned toward Rem and said with a smile, "Rem, not only is it quaint, but it has that storybook Colorado mountain cabin ambiance about it. Do you know what I like most? I like thinking about you as a little boy sitting with your grandpa. I like thinking about you sleeping here and dreaming about what you were going to do when you were a grownup. Thanks for thinking that I am special enough for you to bring me here, Cowboy."

Rem walked up onto the porch with a grin on his face. "Before we start relaxing, I want to take you on a short hike and show you where I used to battle Indians and fight off bears when I was a little boy. My old fort is probably still there."

As he took her hand, guiding her onto the trail, Callie almost started crying as she thought about the reality of her life compared to the dream she was currently living.

Despite her heavy heart, she gave Rem a big smile. "Do you know that you have taught me to see the beauty all around me? I now look at the clouds differently and am amazed at all the colors jumping out at me in the carpet of different grasses. I can hear the songs of all the birds and the chatter of little animals as they do their daily chores for survival. Thank you, sweet man, for making my life larger than it was. For opening my eyes and awakening my senses.

A low roll of thunder rumbled in the distance. Rem stood and said, "Storm's coming in. Let's head back to the cabin."

Callie agreed, "They seem to roll in fast out here. You probably don't want to have dinner with a drowned rat anyway."

Reaching the front porch, they held each other while staring out at the hard downpour of a typical Colorado afternoon shower…always so cleansing and refreshing. The rain brought a coolness to the late afternoon, so Rem started a fire in the old stone fireplace.

"Callie, I am going to be your chef and wine steward tonight. May I get you a glass of wine before dinner?"

She looked up at him and said, "Yes, you may! You have always been my cowboy, and now you are my wine steward and chef. Rem, I hope you know that you are my everything. After we have the wonderful dinner you are making for us, could I convince you to let me provide the dessert?"

After dinner, they sat on the porch swing, listening to the sounds of the cool summer evening. In the nearest pine tree, a hawk was quietly sitting on a branch near its nest looking over at them. The freshness of the earlier rain shower permeated the early evening air. Snuggling more closely to Rem's side, she whispered, "Rem, what do you think that hawk is thinking as he intently studies us?"

After being silent for a few seconds he said, "Callie, Indian lore has it that a hawk will show up when you need guidance from the universe and support from someone larger than you."

Looking into his eyes, Callie softly said, "Rem, I need guidance of what to do. I don't ever want to leave you, but I keep feeling that I will have to leave you somehow, someday."

Not knowing what to say, Rem stood up and squeezed her hand. "Callie, it's getting late, and I think we should head back in case you do get a late-night call."

Callie nodded. As she walked to the pickup, she bent over and picked one of the roses to take with her as a memory of one of the happiest days of her life.

July 13, 1999

Dear Journal,

It's late tonight, but there is no way that I'm going to be able to sleep without describing what happened today.

Rem took me to his grandparents' cabin in Evergreen as a special treat after being apart for so long. Being with him today was by far the most special day we've had together. He is always thinking of ways to make me happy. To be regarded as someone special is something I haven't had for years and years. I felt as if we were a real couple and not just two separate people who dearly cared for each other.

I will never forget our walk together in the mountain meadows. Although it was a warm, sunny day, a hint of coolness signaled the upcoming fall. The late afternoon sun was golden, and the fragrance of pine needles rose from the forest floor. The clouds cast shadows across the meadows and the sunshine lit up the forest as we walked together, feeling like we were a part of nature.

Looking up at the blue Colorado sky, I saw three circling golden eagles giving us a glimpse of what true freedom looks like. They were riding the wind currents in such a free-spirited way... a freedom that humans will never know.

As the afternoon showers blew in over the western ridgelines, Rem and I ran back to the cabin hand-in-hand, laughing and enjoying the fresh scent of pine needles and mountain grasses as it started to rain.

After we settled back in the cabin, my cowboy made me a fabulous steak dinner accompanied by an aged Bordeaux wine. It was perfect. After dinner, as we cuddled on the couch enjoying the fire, I started feeling extremely playful and a little bit naughty.

I whispered in his ear, "Thank you for such a wonderful dinner. I promised you a great dessert, but I just can't give all of myself to you since I'm not really yours." I stood up from the couch, never breaking eye contact with him. He looked at me in such a loving way and said, "Callie, thank you for loving me. We will be together someday, I hope, but only when the time is right for both of us."

Evergreen, Colorado, is located in the foothills about 40 miles from the ranch. It is known as a charming mountain community that people from all over the United States come to visit. Evergreen's beginning dates back to 1859 when a group of families settled there and formed a ranching community. A dam was built on Bear Creek in 1928, creating Evergreen Lake. The downtown area, with its historic Main Street, is bordered by pink rock cliffs on one side and the mountain stream of Bear Creek on the other side. Main Street offers shopping, bistros, patio cafes, live music and rustic B&B's. After the lake was constructed, Evergreen became a summer and winter recreation destination for day trips by Denver residents.

CHAPTER 15
"CAN IT BE WRONG?"

Rem had been gazing at Callie while she put hay and fresh straw in all the stalls before leaving for the evening. He snapped back to attention when his cell phone rang.

"Rem, this is the Douglas County Sheriff's Office. We're calling to let you know that we found a butchered Angus steer in an abandoned construction yard near Palmer Lake. From what's left, it looks like the brand on the hide is yours. The detectives want you to confirm it before they further analyze the crime site."

Rem paused for a moment and looked out at the field. "Thanks, Sheriff. I'll grab my gear and head that way."

The old, rough road going into the site was nearly impossible for vehicles to navigate. Rem packed a first aid kit and survival gear into his saddle bags, saddled Cimarron, and loaded him into his horse trailer.

As Callie finished her chores, she saw Rem loading Cimarron into the horse trailer. "Rem," she shouted, "where are you taking him at this time of day?"

Rem fastened the trailer gate and walked over, explaining that the sheriff's department had called him about a steer that had been slaughtered by poachers down by Palmer Lake. "They think my brand is on the steer's hide."

"Oh, no." Looking up at Rem, Callie said, "Bill's in San Diego tonight, so he won't even know I'm gone. Not that he would notice anyway. I'll ride with you."

"Sounds like a plan," Rem agreed. "Jump in. Let's go."

Rem got in and started up the truck as Callie climbed into the cab and settled into the passenger seat. They looked at each other as Rem put the truck in gear and pushed the gas pedal.

As they drove down Highway 105, Rem thought of all the possible routes to figure out the fastest way to the old Smith place where the rock quarry construction site was located. He remembered there wasn't cell service in that area, which meant the mapping function on his cell phone wouldn't be able to offer any guidance.

As they rode down the highway, they took in the local scenery. The evening temperature was relatively warm, but there was a coolness in the air. Nighttime dew was already forming on the blades of prairie grass. Fortunately, the moon was almost full, so it would act like a beacon guiding Rem's way once he saddled up Cimarron.

Pulling off the highway to the entry of the old quarry pit construction site, Rem turned off the engine, leaned over to give Callie a big kiss, and said, "I need you to stay here. You will be okay because the sheriff's department is sending another car down to watch this entrance. They should be right behind us. If you need anything, blast the horn two times and I will be here before you blink your eyes."

Callie kissed him quickly and assured him, "I know I will be fine, but I can't wait until you get back. So go get your butt in that saddle, Cowboy, before I beg to ride along with you."

Rem rode slowly on the rutted road that wove through the Ponderosa pines. The sound of old twigs cracking under Cimarron's hooves added to the Old West romance of the early evening. The scent of pines in the night air only heightened his visions and emotions. The shadows of the big Ponderosa pines were dancing around the forest floor as a steady, soft evening breeze caressed the long pine boughs. He felt at peace being alone with the feeling of Cimarron moving slowly underneath the saddle. The sensation of being alone in the forest wasn't derived from loneliness. It was a feeling that all was right with the world. The hooting of a Great Horned Owl added to what his eyes and nose were experiencing.

Rem's calm feeling quickly ended when the owl sailed by with a piercing shrill as his six-foot wingspan cut through the air currents. With goosebumps on his arms and a chill down the center of his back, Rem shuddered as he attempted to settle Cimarron down. With the goosebumps still in place, he spotted the butchered steer hanging on a Ponderosa pine branch. Dismounting, he grabbed the reins and led Cimarron over to the carcass. He had no trouble identifying the brand as his. However, even more vexing were the hoofprints from five head of cattle that had been driven back toward the main road. He would need to do a headcount of his herd first thing in the morning.

As Rem returned to the quarry's entrance, he saw a sheriff's car parked next to his truck. The deputy and Callie were chatting as Rem rode up and dismounted.

"I checked things out," Rem reported while walking toward them. "Not only is the butchered steer my brand, but it looks like they might have loaded up five more steers into a trailer. Rick, I would suggest that you put out an alert for all your deputies to keep an eye out for suspicious trailers that probably are not licensed in Douglas County." The deputy agreed to do so and headed toward his car.

Rem opened the passenger door of the truck for Callie and said, "Callie, just down the road is an excellent roadside bar and grill with the best buffalo wings in all of Colorado. I'm really hungry, and I need a beer or two. How about you?"

Smiling, Callie replied, "Rem, I love wings, I love beer, and I love you." Her face flushed as the words had escaped and there was no retracting them. "Start this truck up and let's go."

"Yeah, you love beer. Now that's one we'll have to question." Rem smiled and hugged her close, kissing the top of her head.

After they'd eaten too many wings Rem helped Callie get down from her stool and guided her to the truck. She had enjoyed a few too many beers, too, but Rem had nursed just one.

As the truck headed north, Rem noticed that Callie was beginning to sob. Seeing a trailhead parking area ahead on the right, Rem pulled the truck and trailer in and parked the truck on the far side labeled "Trucks and Trailers Only."

Rem leaned over, pulled Callie closer to his side, and softly asked, "Callie, what's wrong? I have never seen you cry so hard. Talk to me."

Pulling away and trying to open the passenger door of the truck, she shouted, "You don't know a thing about me! I'm a terrible person, and I don't deserve to be loved by anyone. I fake people out like I've done with you and Bill and all my friends. I lie, and I am deceitful. Is that who you want to be with? I think I am going to be sick, so open the window NOW."

Rem opened the window and helped Callie get her head out. After throwing up while fat tears rolled down her flushed cheeks, she fell back on the seat exhausted. Rem sat back quietly, thinking that the next move needed to be hers and not his.

Looking over and apologizing for getting sick, Callie said, "I have some things to tell you, and I don't want you to say a word until I'm done.

"Before I met you, I was not a very good judge of character in men. In high school my boyfriend kept pushing me to have sex. I finally gave in, and the next day he told all his friends, and I quote, 'I not only nailed her, but I nailed her good, and now I'm on to college to find more chicks.' I was humiliated and did not date during the rest of my senior year.

"In college, I started dating Bill, who seemed like someone I could marry. Actually, I found him boring and aloof to be around. I did not want to be in the dating scene, so being with him seemed okay.

"After we were engaged, he did not have any time for me because he was studying around the clock to get ready for the Medical Boards. To occupy myself, I joined a workout club with some of my girlfriends. The club's manager took an interest in me and started helping me with my routines. I craved the attention, since I wasn't getting any from Bill. One night we went out for some beers and then he wanted to go into the club to get something. I followed him into his office, and he grabbed me and told me how much I turned him on. I let him seduce me, and we ended up having sex on the floor. I never returned to the club after that night. "Months later, I discovered I was pregnant, and I thought it might be Rick's baby. I let Bill know I was pregnant and told him we needed to get married right away. I couldn't bring myself to take a test to see who the father really was."

Callie frowned, her eyes fixed on her hands in her lap. "So, Cowboy, I'm not worthy of your love. In fact, I'm not even capable of loving myself."

"Callie," Rem said softly as he reached across the console to place his hand gently over hers. "I did not interrupt you as you requested, and now I need ask you to do the same for me…agreed?" Callie nodded. "First of all, I want to talk about your feelings of being unworthy of love because of how you behaved. Don't you see that your high school boyfriend and gym manager took advantage of you? They, not you, should feel guilty about how they treated you. Your boyfriend led you on about how he felt about you. He deceived you and hurt you intentionally. The gym manager wanted to seduce you from the day he met you. The night you had a couple of beers with him was innocent in your mind, but he knew what he was trying to accomplish. You can't completely blame yourself because you don't even have any idea if he drugged your beers. My thought is that he did because you were so compliant. Think about it, Callie: except for Bill, you've only had sex twice in your whole life."

Reaching over to hug her, he said, "I guess there isn't any better time to tell you something that has haunted me my entire life. I have never told another living soul about it until now.

"When I was a senior at Princeton, I began drinking heavily. As a result, I started missing classes, and my grades were a disaster. It became so bad that there was no way I would graduate in May since I had an F in two classes and needed those credits to graduate.

"I had been dating Sandy, who worked in the Registrar's office. One of her jobs was to download all the professors' test papers onto a very secure server and then print them on the day of testing. One weekend, I took her skiing and told her I was struggling in school and probably would not be able to graduate in May. I asked her if she could give me the tests and answers for the two classes I was failing. She said she'd think about it, but she didn't want to risk being caught.

"Then Sandy started crying as she told me about problems that made mine look like nothing. Her father had recently had a heart attack, and the medical bills had pretty much wiped out what she needed for tuition, so she would have to drop out of school. I felt sorry for her, and wanted to help her.

"I had inherited a large sum of money when my grandparents passed away, so I secretly paid her tuition. Then somehow, magically, my grades changed to passing grades. It had to have been her that changed my grades. To this day, I can't believe I just let that happen and I do feel deep guilt and shame for rolling with it.

"Callie, even though we are both sorry for what we did, we still deserve to move on…to be happy and to be loved. I appreciate that you felt safe enough to disclose all that information with me. I am fortunate to have the opportunity to understand where you're coming from. Oh, and one more thing: I love you even more after hearing what you've gone through!"

CHAPTER 16
AND THE MOON WAS FULL

As Rem pulled out of the parking area and turned the truck onto Highway 105, Callie snuggled up to him and said, "Rem, you are so understanding. Your words have brought great comfort to my soul."

With the full moon so bright, the foothills were illuminated to the point where the hills and valleys were as clear as day. Suddenly a coyote ran across the road, causing Rem to brake hard, but not hard enough to cause Cimarron to fall in the trailer. He shook his head and rubbed his eyes, noticing that Callie had fallen asleep on his shoulder.

She woke as Rem pulled into the yard by his house. He looked at Callie and said, "Do you mind staying here in the house for a few minutes while I check on the horses down at the barn?"

"Of course not; just stay safe and hurry back," Callie instructed.

When he returned, he saw Callie's car but could not locate her when he entered the house. He called out, "Where is my little angel?" Not hearing anything, he walked into his study, the soft glow of a lamp casting warm light over the room. Callie was curled up in one of his big cowhide leather chairs, wrapped snugly in his Pendleton blanket. The faint scent of leather mixed with the comforting warmth of the fire in the hearth as he knelt beside her, brushing a stray strand of hair from her cheek. Dropping to his knees in front of the chair he smiled and whispered to her, "How is my angel doing?"

"Rem, I am only your borrowed angel. Today in the barn, I was cleaning your saddle when the song 'Borrowed Angel' was playing on the radio. Have you ever heard the song?"

Rem shook his head, a faint smile tugging at his lips as he thought about how much Callie's words resonated with his own feelings.

"Well, let me tell you a couple of the verses," Callie offered. "I think it went like this:

Borrowed angels belong to someone else.
I love my borrowed angel,
I just can't help myself.
That ring upon her finger don't belong to me.
But she loves me, and I know she'll save
Some borrowed time for me.

"Rem, I am so torn, and I don't know what to do next. I may not be back after tonight since I have a lot to figure out and think about," she said, her voice trembling. Callie glanced away, twisting her hands in her lap as if trying to hold herself together.

"Now, hold me like I'm dying, because I need what might just be our last embrace. I want you to make love to me like couples do when it is their first time and could be their last time, but I can't.

"So, let me breathe you in so you will be in my soul forever. Now, close your eyes and fly with your angel to a cloud that you have never ridden on before."

With tears forming in his eyes, Rem spoke into her ear, "Sweet angel, my life has been made so complete knowing, touching, and sharing with you. If I died tonight, I could ask for no more on this earth. No matter what the future holds, you will live in my heart until the end of my time."

Exhausted by emotions of an intensity she'd never felt before, Callie fell asleep in the arms of her cowboy.

July 2, 1999

Dear Journal,

Instead of a glass of wine, I am going to pour a cup of hot coffee and curl up under my throw blanket so I can write about last night... the first night Rem and I spent together.

How could I say, "Rem, I may never be back to see you again?" and then experience the most intimate emotional moment a girl only dreams about?

After hearing Rem's words and seeing the tears in his eyes, I felt like I had found the man I'd always dreamed of. Being with Rem has always taken me to another place, but last night was a total out-of-body experience.

How can I not spend the rest of my life with this man who owns my heart and my soul? Why can't I decide what to do?

I think I know why, but I just don't want to think about it or even write about it. Why can't I dismiss the past and move on with life?

Can I move on from the past and accept that I deserve having Rem in my life forever? Or will I continue to be the young girl who believed I didn't deserve to be happy after what I did.

Say it out loud, Callie! Write it down on paper, Callie! Scream it out the window, Callie! Tell the world, Callie!

Dear Journal,

I'm finally putting pen to paper about the darkness I've carried for so long, and it's already overwhelming. My hands are shaking, my eyes are blurry from tears, and honestly, I'm considering digging out that hidden pack of cigarettes I haven't touched in years. Maybe even adding Bailey's to my coffee. Anything to calm the storm inside me.

It's time to confront the truth I've been too afraid to face. There's so much sadness and guilt tied to the choices I've made. I don't feel like I deserve to be happy or to be with Rem because of the lie I've been living. I never told Bill that Ben might not be his son. Last night, I told Rem about the one-night affair that could have led to my pregnancy. How could I marry Bill knowing this? I told myself I was protecting everyone—Bill, Ben, our family—but really, I was hiding. And the lie has haunted me ever since. How could I have done that?

But that's not even the worst of it. Just before my mom died, she revealed something that shattered me. Bill knew. He had done a DNA test when the boys were young and discovered Ben wasn't his biological son. He kept it a secret—not out of love, but out of fear and selfishness. He was terrified of losing half of what he'd earned if we got divorced. He even threatened my mom, making her promise not to tell me. He said if the truth came out, he'd ruin me—tell my son I was a whore and destroy our family.

Hearing that broke me. I spent years carrying this guilt, thinking I'd wronged Bill so deeply, only to find out he used my mistake to manipulate me. My mom apologized before she died, saying she regretted not telling me sooner and making me feel like I had to stay married. I forgave her because I could see how scared she'd been, but the anger I feel toward Bill is consuming.

Now my heart is with Rem, trying to embrace the love we've found, but the past feels like an anchor. How can I let myself be happy when I feel so unworthy? Can I move forward, or am I destined to carry this weight forever?

For now, I'll keep writing. Maybe these pages will help me find a way out of the shadows.

Love,
Callie

CHAPTER 17
OH, NO!

When Callie did not arrive at the barn the next morning, Rem started to worry. As he began to feed the horses, his cell phone rang.

"Rem, this is Callie. Sorry I couldn't call you earlier, but I was with Bill until now. I have a doctor's appointment, so I won't be out to the ranch today. I only have an hour available tomorrow, but I need to see you. Can I just meet you where we usually do on that gravel road south of Sedalia? I can't talk any longer, so I will see you in the morning."

For several weeks, Callie had been worried that she might have breast cancer. She had found a lump in her left breast while doing a routine self-exam. She was especially worried because her mother and sister had both been breast cancer survivors.

Since her mom was no longer around, Callie called her sister Beth for moral support and advice.

"Call your primary care physician today and let him know that you need to see him as soon as possible," Beth insisted. "He will do a blood work screen on you and send you to the hospital for a biopsy. I love you, Sis, and you are going to be okay."

Beth did her best to reassure Callie as she continued, "As you know, our mom had to have a double mastectomy, but I did not. I will start praying for you, but promise me that you will call the doctor today, okay?"

Callie softly uttered, "Beth, I will call today, and thank you for your prayers."

A week after the biopsy was taken, the oncology department at Littleton Adventist Hospital called Callie to set up an appointment with Dr. Hadid. When Bill and Callie arrived at the Cancer Center at Littleton Adventist Hospital, Dr. Hadid ushered them into his office and asked them to sit down.

Opening the folder on his desk, the doctor said, "Tests show that you have breast cancer, Callie. It's advanced—more advanced than I was expecting. It's bilateral, Mrs. Parker. Pretty rare."

"Oh. Oh, I see. Both? Uh, wow. Dr. Hadid, could you repeat that? I think I misheard you," Callie said, her voice quiet, but determined to hear something else. She looked at Bill, who had leaned over the desk to see what was written on the file. Dr. Hadid closed the file, and Bill sat back, looking up at the top of the wall and resting his hands on his thighs. Callie reached for Bill's hand as he folded his arms. She looked back at the doctor and said again, "Dr. Hadid. Um. Can you…."

Dr. Hadid leaned forward, "Callie, the sooner we start treatment, the better the outcome. I recommend a complete mastectomy, followed by chemotherapy. I have an opening on Thursday for your surgery. Can you make that work? You need to make it work."

Bill said, "Callie, Dr. Hadid is right. Schedule surgery for Thursday."

Callie looked at both men and then calmly said, "I want to proceed with the surgery on Thursday. I don't want to wait. Bill, don't tell the boys until I'm out of surgery and you can tell them that I'm okay. I will call Beth and let her know what my diagnosis is."

In the car on the way home, Bill told Callie, "I can be with you on Thursday, but you know I have to be out of town on Friday. I will catch the red eye Thursday night and try to get back Saturday morning. It's too late for me to cancel this seminar with over 300 surgeons coming to hear me speak. It's important. I'll hire a full-time nurse after you are discharged and sent home. That will be easiest."

"Bill, don't worry about it. I'm sure I will be fine. I will be heavily sedated in recovery, so I won't even know you are not there."

As Callie spoke, all she could think about was Rem. If Rem could have been with her, he would not have even left the hospital to go home to sleep. She needed a big hug and a strong voice reassuring her that everything would be okay. She looked out the car window and realized that Bill had offered neither.

September 5, 1999

Dear Journal,

My stomach is in knots tonight. My heart feels like it is being torn apart. I can't stop crying as I write this.

I am worried about the kids and how they will react. My sons are strong, but this is a whole different ballgame. I'm not sure they will be much help. Lord knows Bill won't give a crap. He'll expect everything to be just like normal by Monday. Ha. Not even kidding. I have a lot to figure out for sure.

But Dear Journal, The past five months have been so beautiful. My heart and soul are so filled with love. I think back to the moments we shared, the days when we escaped from the world and spent time together. Whether we were lying in each other's arms talking and laughing or holding each other close— it didn't matter. Everything was right with the world.

But tomorrow I need to say goodbye to Rem. I suspected the time would come when we might have to say our goodbyes, but I never wanted to believe it would happen. I must leave him now, but I can't tell him about my breast cancer diagnosis before I go. It breaks my heart knowing that I can't be open and truthful with him.

CHAPTER 18
SAY GOODBYE

Rem had never figured out how those moments in life work when you wake up like it's any other day and then a life-changing event takes place that makes you wish you could go back to the past.

As he parked his pickup truck in the pine trees a few hundred yards off the gravel road where he was to meet Callie, he lowered the window and took in a deep breath. Breathing in the smell of country air on an early September fall morning always did so much for his soul. As always, he was longing to see Callie's lovely face and hear her calming voice.

On her way to meet Rem, Callie pulled her car over to the side of the road. She re-applied her lipstick and eyeliner because she had been crying all morning. Between her upcoming surgery and saying goodbye to Rem, she wasn't sure how she was even capable of driving. Her nerves were frayed, and her heart felt like it had broken into a million pieces. A smile crossed her lips as she predicted that Rem would have a hot cup of coffee waiting for her.

Seeing that he had already arrived, she pulled up to his back bumper. Not daring to hesitate, she jumped out of her car and headed for the passenger door of his pick-up. Before jumping in, she took a very deep breath and feigned a big smile.

Before she could talk, he took her hand, leaned over, and gave her one of those kisses a woman can't ever forget.

She pulled back after the kiss and softly said, "We should talk. Rem, we can't continue on like this. You know this, too. To disappoint our families would kill us both because of who we are. You're a courageous and honorable man. I have to say goodbye today. But maybe a fortuitous moment will bring us together again sometime down the road.

"Unless it is fortuitous, I don't want you to reach out to me, nor I to you. I will leave you today with a smile and this statement." She smiled, taking his hand in hers and intertwining their fingers as she continued speaking.

"Rem, all my life I have wondered what it would be like to really love a man before I die. And now I know, so thank you for making my dream come true. I love you so much, and I'm prepared to take that secret to the grave with me."

Rem cleared his throat, considering his words carefully as he thought about how to respond. Before he could say anything, Callie jumped out of the truck and ran to her car. Without Rem seeing, she had slipped a note down between the seat cushions in his pickup.

Watching through his rearview mirror, Rem could barely process what had just happened as he watched Callie climb into her vehicle and throw her car into reverse. He knew Callie well enough to know not to chase after her, no matter how desperately his heart cried out for him to move. He wanted to chase after her, but his legs felt like rubber. He could not and did not want to climb out of the truck and watch her drive out of his life. He knew she'd meant every word she had spoken, and he would not see her again. How could that be possible?

For the next hour, he could not move. With his arms propped up against the steering wheel, he closed his eyes and tried to imagine living without her. From that day forward, he knew he would have a heartache that would last forever. His mind replayed her words in his head like a broken record: "Rem, all my life, I have wondered what it would be like to really love a man before I die." If she felt that way, why would she say goodbye? If other people could fight through divorce issues, weren't he and Callie strong enough to do so? How could he exist without her in his life? Then he remembered how his dad always said, "To survive, you have to let go…it is part of moving forward."

Before Callie jumped out of the truck, he had been planning to let her know that he had just received a FedEx envelope from Jane with divorce papers to be signed by him. He was proud that he hadn't initially said anything, since that would have been unfair to Callie. Even with that knowledge, she would have still faced the same issues. It would have been so selfish of him to do so. But… had he made a mistake?

September 5, 1999

Dear Journal,

I barely held myself together today. I didn't even know if I would be strong enough to say goodbye. Before I could say anything, he leaned forward and gave me a long, lingering kiss. It was as if he already knew.

My heart was breaking as I inhaled the scent of him. I wanted to remember everything about him...the way he smelled, the way he felt, the way he looked at me, the way he made me laugh. Most of all, the way he made me feel.

When I got out of the truck and closed the door, it took everything I had not to look back. I didn't dare turn around because I wouldn't be able to control the tears if I saw his face. I love that man so much. I'm happy that I will have such wonderful memories, but it is those memories that make saying goodbye so hard.

I know what I am doing is the right thing, but it sure doesn't feel that way. I wanted to tell him about my cancer diagnosis, but it would not have been fair to put that burden on him. It's me and my family who must deal with this. I know he would be there for me, but like he said to me a while back, "Callie, I wish you were mine." I do too... but I'm not!!!!!

CHAPTER 19
AND TIME MARCHES ON

Not a day went by when Rem did not think about Callie. Had she made the right decision for their lives? Probably not, but it was the right decision for the lives of others she loved.

The hole in his heart remained as empty as the day they'd said goodbye. He had discovered the note she'd tucked away in the seat cushions of the truck. It was so sad. It described how their time together was like Garth Brooks' song "The Dance."

Callie's note read:

Dear Rem,

I am sure Garth Brooks had us in mind when he wrote "The Dance." Like the song said, "Before meeting you, never in my life did I feel the world was right." The Dance we shared allowed me to feel freedom and romantic love for the first time. I would never have guessed that it would be me who said goodbye. You were my everything and always will be. The pain I feel is beyond words, but I will replace the pain knowing that I did not miss the dance.

Thank you, Cowboy!

Six months after he last saw Callie, Rem received a call in the middle of the night from the Colorado State Highway Patrol.

The dispatcher said that Wade had been in a terrible car accident on Highway 119 heading into the mountains. It appeared he had been heading to Black Hawk where he spent much of his time gambling. He had been dating and living with a woman who owned a retail flower shop close to the Lady Luck Casino in Black Hawk.

Ever since Wade had lost the two ranches, his drinking had been out of control. The dispatcher said he'd missed a curve and his pickup went over the edge of the narrow highway. "His truck tumbled down the cliff, rolling multiple times before finally landing in North Clear Creek."

The dispatcher then told Rem that a Flight for Life helicopter had taken Wade to St. Anthony's Hospital off of Union and 6th Avenue in Lakewood.

After throwing on some clothes, Rem jumped into his pickup and headed to Sedalia, where he turned north on Highway 85. When he arrived at the hospital, he rushed to the Emergency Room entrance. After giving his name to the receptionist, he headed to the coffee machine and pressed the button for coffee with cream. He grabbed the coffee from the dispenser and huffed, "No cream," and found a chair where he would wait for his name to be called. After a few minutes, an attending physician came out and informed him that Wade had passed away.

Since Wade had been a tortured soul in so many ways during his lifetime, Rem said a prayer that their mother was able to comfort Wade as he passed into the afterlife to be with her. They had always been so close, and now they would be together again.

It was up to Rem to make funeral arrangements since the woman Wade was living with was not his wife. He discovered that her name was Sally. Rem had difficulty communicating with her. From what he learned from others in the community, Sally, like Wade, was an alcoholic. She gave him permission to go to their apartment to gather Wade's belongings. When he asked her if she wanted anything of Wade's, she said no. That response alone sealed the deal for Rem. She was the type of woman who made it easy to dislike her.

After Sally gave him the key, Rem walked up the stairs above the flower shop and unlocked the door to Wade's apartment. He had brought some cardboard boxes with him so he could collect Wade's possessions. He started to sort through items to keep and items to give to Goodwill.

After piling all of Wade's clothes and boots in the Goodwill boxes, he spotted a suitcase under the bed. Pulling it out, he saw that it was locked with a good-sized padlock.

After getting a large bolt cutter out of his pickup, he cut the lock with little effort. Opening the suitcase caused him to step back and take a deep breath. The suitcase was filled with sentimental pictures of their mom and dad. Whether Wade was drunk or just sad when he wrote them, he had oodles of handwritten notes scattered among the pictures. They were notes of apology for his behavior as a child and for who he had become when their dad was still alive. There were notes to Mom about her dying so young and leaving him all alone. There was even an envelope addressed to Rem labeled "Only open upon my death." He then found another envelope that was labeled Last Will & Testament. Like the other notes, it was handwritten.

He opened the envelope and read aloud:

LAST WILL & TESTAMENT OF
WADE CUNNINGHAM

I, Wade Cunningham, a resident of Gilpin County, Colorado, revoke any prior wills and codicils made by me and declare this my Will.

I am a single man with no children.

I appoint Remington Cunningham to be my personal representative and grant him all powers to dispose of my estate and grant my last wishes as listed herein below:

1. Transfer any money I may have in my checking account as well as the title to my truck to Sally Bergman.

2. I wish to be cremated with my ashes spread on top of my mother's grave at the Castle Rock Cemetery.

3. I would like Father Ed Flanigan (who I think lives in Montana at this time) to officiate the funeral with only my brother Rem present.

I, Wade Cunningham, sign and execute this instrument on this __day of ___, 200_ as my Will, that I sign it willingly, that I execute it as my free and voluntary act for the purposes expressed herein. I am eighteen years of age or older, of sound mind, and under no constraint or undue influence.

Wade Cunningham

After getting into his truck, Rem remembered the envelope labeled "Only open upon my death." He ripped it open, removed the handwritten letter, and started reading it.

Dear Rem,

With both my stepfather and me gone from this earth, there is something I must tell you even though it will hurt you. I promised Dad that I would never tell you what happened between me and him, but now I feel I must explain myself to you. As little boys, you and I loved each other as much as full brothers love each other. I so admired who you were and what you accomplished.

After Mom died, you noticed that I became a different person. A person you did not like nor respect. Most everyone thought I could not accept her death, but something else happened.

One night when you were gone, I went down to the barn to see if I could help Dad. When I opened the door to the tack room, he was quite drunk and sobbing into his hands. Concerned and scared, I said, "What's wrong, Dad? Are you okay?" Seeing it was me, he said, "I cannot live with this secret any longer." I knelt beside him and whispered, "What secret is bothering you so much?" With a shortness to his breath and gasping for air since he was still crying, he said, "I am not the hero everyone thinks I am. The hero was really your father. I was supposed to be flying in the left chair the day we met with enemy fire. Your dad said for me to go check on all the gunners and he would fly us into the zone to be bombed. I wasn't in the cockpit when the bullets came through the glass and fuselage. I should have told everyone this real story and made sure your dad received a medal instead of me."

Rem, with my bad temper, I screamed at him, "So, you took his life, you took his wife, and you took his child. How can you even look at yourself?" I apologized later, but things were never the same between us. He kept trying to do things for me, but nothing really worked. Didn't you ever wonder or question why I was named Executor to his will?

I should have been stronger but that was always your role. Thanks for continuing to look out for me and for the love you showed to me.

Wade

With his parents and brother gone, his sons living on their own, and Callie no longer with him, Rem had fought depression for quite some time. After the funeral service for Wade, he decided that for his own mental health, it would be best if he got off the ranch for a while. He decided to join a couple of organizations in Castle Rock. He became a member of the Douglas County Fair Board and was appointed to chair the annual rodeo at the Douglas County Fair.

Not only did he enjoy setting up the rodeo events, but he was also meeting more women than he could ever imagine. He would shake his head sometimes when he tried to figure out what in the hell he was trying to accomplish by dating different women. Some of the women owned a horse, some had never ridden a horse, some were short, and some were tall. There were blondes and brunettes, full-figured or slender. Some were attorneys, some were waitresses, and one was a well-known senator. The relationship never seemed to go deeper than the surface. A calming voice, but no sparkling eyes; or a beautiful smile, but no sense of playfulness. Why was he unable to find another love?

CHAPTER 20
NOT ME IN THE MIRROR

Even though being on the Douglas County Fair Board was gratifying, Rem still could not fill the emptiness in his life. It had been years since he had last seen Callie, but not a day went by when he didn't think about her.

Waking up one morning, he looked into the bathroom mirror and whispered to himself, "My life no longer resembles me." He thought about what he could do to get back on track with who he truly was. He needed to appreciate what he had going for himself instead of focusing on his losses.

He gripped the counter tightly as he looked into the mirror. He told his reflection, "Rem, get ahold of yourself. We are all victims of the past. That was then, and this is now." He decided that he needed an adventure that would test his resolve, spirit, and physical prowess.

He had always wanted to pack into northern Montana on horseback. Being a lover of western pioneer history, he wanted to experience what the famous cowboys and mountain men had experienced over 100 years ago… real men like Jim Bridger, John Colter, Buffalo Bill Cody, and Kit Carson.

After telling his son Jack and his ranch foreman Caleb that he was going to take a horseback pack trip into the Bob Marshall Wilderness in northern Montana, he started packing his gear for the trip. Jack was concerned that he was going alone and tried to persuade him to take one of his friends from the Fair Board. Looking at Jack, he said, "Son, this trip isn't just an adventure. It's about figuring out who I am again."

He had picked the Bob Marshall Wilderness area for several reasons. Bob had been to the ranch when Rem was growing up, since he was a friend of Rem's dad. The Wilderness Act of 1964 was passed by Congress to protect the natural conditions of wilderness while providing the use of the area to the public. The area is populated by grizzly bears, lynx, wolverines, deer, elk, gray wolves, moose, black bears, mountain lions, and mountain sheep. There are over 1700 miles of trails, with the Continental Divide running through the middle of the wilderness area.

As Rem backed up his pickup, Jack and Caleb helped hitch the fifth-wheel four-horse trailer to the truck. Rem had decided to take the larger trailer since he was bringing Cimarron and also taking Chief to be a pack horse. The four-horse trailer provided enough room to take bales of hay and sacks of oats. It also came equipped with its own sleeping loft. When he was traveling long distances, he liked to stay near the horses overnight.

Waving goodbye to Jack and Caleb, he drove out of the ranch gate and headed to I-25 at Castle Rock. As he headed north toward Denver, his cell phone rang and the caller ID identified Katherine, who lived in Estes Park and was married to his fraternity brother Chet.

Putting his cell phone on speaker, he shouted out over the highway noise, "Hi, Katherine, how are you?"

With a quivering voice, Katherine said, "Rem, I am so scared for Chet, and I didn't know who else to call. Can you talk right now?"

Rem replied, "Sure, Katherine. I'm driving toward Denver right now, heading to Montana. What is going on?"

Katherine explained, "Chet is in New York right now, meeting with Ted to see if he will refinance the ranch for us. I'm afraid that for a number of reasons, Ted is going to call the loan and foreclose on the ranch. It is very serious and scary, Rem."

"Katherine, I can tell you are very, very upset. I'm heading north right now, so I will take the Longmont exit and head over to Estes Park so we can talk in person, okay?"

Hardly able to contain her emotions, Katherine whispered, "Thank you, Rem. I will see you in a couple of hours. Oh, hey, be careful of mountain lions. A guy got killed the other day."

Rem pulled into the gate of the ranch just outside of Estes Park, and decided to drive down to the barn to unload the horses before heading up to the ranch house. Rem led the horses into the barn and found two empty stalls. He took off their halters and filled the mangers with fresh mountain timothy hay, and walked down the barn alleyway, noticing that all the other stalls were empty. He looked out into the paddock area, he was surprised to see that there weren't any horses there either.

Rem retrieved his saddle bag briefcase from the truck, he walked up to the front door of the house. After he knocked, Katherine came to the door with tears in her eyes. She immediately said, "Rem, come in and sit while I fix you a drink. If I remember correctly, you always drink Crown Royal straight up. I will get you your drink and my double scotch."

Smiling, Rem remarked, "Sounds like a perfect way to start a conversation. Oh, by the way, why did I not see your Polo ponies down at the barn?" Instead of answering his question, Katherine started crying.

One of Rem's eyebrows raised inquisitively as he watched her weep. He stood up from the chair he had just sat down in and then approached her. "What did I say, Katherine? What in the hell is going on? Come and talk to me. I will finish getting the drinks."

After taking a long sip of her scotch, Katherine leaned forward with her hands on her knees and said, "Rem, we are caught up in the financial crisis in a devastating way. One of the banks has already taken our horses, and a foreclosure notice has been filed on the ranch. Chet had invested our money in New York with Lehman Brothers,

Goldman Sachs, and a hedge fund that I can't recall the name of. A couple of days ago, Chet flew to New York City to see if he could salvage any of the investments we were involved in. He called me last night and said it doesn't look good. He is not getting much cooperation from the bankers, and he is worried about FDIC protection since it looks like a lot of shady dealings are going on."

Katherine slowly rose to her feet and said, "Rem, I know it's early in the day, but I need another drink before I can tell you something."

After pouring her drink, she sat across from Rem. She took a long sip, then looked into his eyes, and with a hitch in her voice, said, "One night at one of the fraternity parties, I got very drunk, and Chet took me up to his room to sleep if off. All of a sudden, I started waking up and found a man taking off my pants and rolling me onto my back. I tried to push him away, but I was pinned down on the bed. When he got on top of me, I saw that the man holding me down was Ted. I begged him to stop, but he proceeded to assault me. After he was finished, he grabbed me roughly and said, 'I hope you know if you tell anyone, Chet will quit dating you, and you will never marry him. He won't want damaged goods, especially when I tell everyone how horny you were.'"

Katherine continued, "Just recently, at a sorority reunion, I learned one night after some heavy drinking that Ted had also raped two of my sorority sisters the same way he raped me. Katie and Carol stayed quiet because they didn't want to lose their boyfriends. Since both of them are now divorced, they said that if I ever wanted to go after Ted, they would both join in with me."

With tears in his eyes and a soft voice, Rem replied, "Katherine, I'm so sorry to hear that story. I never had any idea that Ted had behaved this way. I recommend that you do not tell Chet this story. For too many years, you avoided telling him, and he will resent that you did not share it with him. It could destroy what you have. But don't worry, I have an idea of how we can make Ted pay for this. Instead of you and the other girls taking action against him, let me handle this for you."

"Oh, Rem, thank you so much," Katherine said with a sigh of relief.

With a drink in his hand, Rem stood up and said, "Katherine, let's go call Chet right now."

Quick to agree, Katherine called Chet. "Hi, honey, guess who I am visiting with right now?" Katherine said.

Chet replied, "I'm not really in the mood for guessing games right now, so just tell me."

"Rem is here. I called him when I was upset after hearing from you. He was on his way to Montana when I called, so he headed over here since he could tell I was a basket case. We had a great talk. Let me put him on the phone, okay?"

Rem took the phone. "Chet, I'm so sorry to hear about everything that's happening with you and Katherine. How was your meeting with Ted today?"

Chet replied, "It was not good. I just can't understand where he is coming from! If I didn't know better, I would say he wants our ranch for his own. He told me in no uncertain terms that he has no intention of extending the loan and will proceed with foreclosure. I stared at him without saying anything and then walked out of his office. I just called the airlines to book a flight out tonight."

Rem responded, "Chet, cancel that flight for one more day. I will call Ted tomorrow and convince him to change his mind. I have some information that might persuade him, and more than likely, make him unemployable in the future. Call his secretary tomorrow afternoon. She will have loan papers for you to sign, and I'm almost certain you will like the terms of the loan extension."

"Rem, I don't know what you are going to do, but I want to thank you from the bottom of my heart. You are a true friend and brother."

After the phone call to Chet, Katherine and Rem had a nice dinner of Angus beef tips over egg noodles, accompanied by a bottle of Burgundy.

After dinner, Rem told Katherine, "I am going to drive out about 4:30 a.m. and head over towards Longs Peak to see if I can find the mountain lion that killed that hiker. I don't want to wake you, so I'm going to sleep in my trailer loft and be close to the horses. Thank you for a wonderful dinner."

Katherine replied, "Rem, stop here when you get back from hunting that lion. I need to know you are okay, and

I will have lunch or dinner ready for you, depending on when you return."

Early the following morning, Rem loaded the horses into the trailer and headed toward Longs Peak. The scenery created by the mountain ranges was beautiful, but he was preoccupied with figuring out what he was going to say to Ted.

Rem passed Cabin Creek and remembered his dad bringing him and Wade to Estes Park when they were little boys. The fishing had been great, but the time around the campfire was even more special. He could still see his dad teaching them to clean trout, and he could smell the fish cooking in a black skillet over the fire. Then, in the morning, the mouth-watering smell of bacon frying permeated the whole area. He still missed his dad after all these years.

As Rem drove, the weight of his unhappiness settled heavily on him. Since the last time he saw Callie, he'd been unable to understand how he had lost her so suddenly. Hadn't she been just as happy as he was? The loneliness gnawed at him, leaving him aching for her, convinced that no other woman could ever fill the void she left. He had let his "poor me" feelings fester, spiraling into a suffocating depression that left him broken and unable to move forward. If he didn't find a way to shift his mindset, the anger simmering inside him would take over. Maybe the wilderness held the clarity he so desperately needed.

After parking his truck and trailer at a local riding stable, he saddled Cimarron and secured his gear on Chief's packing rig. Mounting Cimarron, he headed out toward Longs Peak.

As he rode along, he thought about his life and the anger issues that plagued him. He really needed to pull up on his bootstraps and start living again. He had always been a very rational yet compassionate person who was also profoundly philosophical. In the past, he had always achieved his goals and dreams using perseverance to overcome obstacles that stood in his way. He believed the most significant achievement in life was to find peace of mind. Not only to find it, but to retain and enjoy it.

His dad used to tell him, "Understand that you have to play the hand you are dealt. Live your life like it is a card game. It is all about the choices you make. You can choose to be happy, or you can choose to be sad. You have the free will to make that decision. It is up to you. Don't let anyone else control your happiness."

With a smile, Rem looked up at the beautiful blue sky. "Thanks, Dad."

Toward late afternoon, he brought the horses to a standstill and gazed at the Chasm Lake basin. It looked so peaceful and beautiful. The meadow before him appeared pastoral, with the mountain grasses waving in the gentle breeze. The shadows from the rising sun were slowly creeping down the cliffs surrounding the valley. The sun painted a spectrum of colors as it reflected off the aspen leaves and the towering pines.

After giving the horses a breather, Rem made his way down to the meadow floor. There, he noticed what appeared to be mountain lion tracks. Dismounting from Cimarron to get a closer look, he studied the size of the paw print and knew it had been made by an enormous older lion.

The horses were munching on the delicious mountain grass, but now their heads had turned to the left and their ears were perked up. As he prepared to remount, Cimarron began sidestepping and snorting. Chief's eyes were wild-looking, and his nostrils were flared. Rem was sure that they could both smell the lion.

Leaping onto Cimarron's back by grabbing the saddle horn without using the stirrup, he grabbed his Winchester from the scabbard and laid it across his lap. Chief started bucking and pulling so hard that the pack saddle flew off. He then took off running across the valley.

Cimarron began to buck so hard that Rem figured it would be safer to jump off than fall off. With the Winchester in hand, he leaped toward the higher incline side of the hill in case Cimarron fell and rolled over on top of him.

The massive mountain lion loped toward them with startling speed, catching Rem off guard. Its powerful paw shot out in a blur, striking Cimarron with a force only a predator of that size could deliver. The claws tore deep, leaving a gaping wound that erupted with blood. Cimarron crumpled to the ground instantly, helpless and unmoving.

Rem's instinct screamed at him to stay, to fight for Cimarron—but he knew he only had moments. He turned to gain distance, but it wasn't enough. The blood-soaked lion, eyes wild, bounded up the hill, locking onto him.

Rem's heart pounded. He couldn't outrun a 180-pound mountain lion, so he stopped suddenly, spinning to face the predator, then bracing himself. The lion let out a deafening growl, and launched itself through the air, claws extended.

There was no time to think—only to act. Rem's training flashed in his mind: the only sure way to stop a charging lion was a single, perfect shot, straight between the eyes.

This was his one chance to survive.

From about 20 yards away, Rem aimed his lever-action Winchester and fired one shot that hit the lion in the shoulder but was not a kill shot. When he went to load another round, the lever action jammed, preventing a new round from entering the chamber. The lion was wounded but still coming toward him. Rem jumped behind a tree and frantically worked the jammed gun. When the lever action cocked again, he used the tree to steady his aim and then fired five rounds into the lion at close range. The lion collapsed instantly, dying only feet away from the tree.

Rem slumped against the base of an aspen tree, his chest heaving as he fought to catch his breath. For a long moment, he stared at the lifeless beast sprawled nearby, his mind reeling. Then, a raw, guttural roar tore from his throat—a mix of triumph, rage, and exhaustion.

With shaking hands, he reached for the Bowie knife at his side, the blade gleaming as he pulled it from its sheath. He knelt beside the lion, his movements precise, and sliced cleanly, severing one of its three-inch claws. The trophy gleamed in his palm, a stark reminder of the battle that had nearly claimed his life.

Rem made his way down the hill to where Cimarron lay still and lifeless. Kneeling beside him, Rem placed a trembling hand on his horse's coat, then leaned in close, listening for a heartbeat that wasn't there. The silence was heavy, final.

Lowering his head, Rem whispered a prayer of thanksgiving—gratitude for the years he'd shared with his faithful companion and for sparing his own life.

"Cimarron," he said softly, his voice thick with emotion, "You and I have been through so much. Thank you, my friend." He held the lion's claw in his palm and gazed at it, his resolve firm. "This will remind me not to be angry, not to be unhappy, and most of all, to treat every day as a blessing from God."

With care, Rem removed the bridle and saddle from his beloved horse, each movement deliberate, reverent. He paused to run a hand down Cimarron's muzzle one last time. "I will miss you, my friend," he whispered. Then he stood, the weight of loss heavy on his shoulders, and looked out across the quiet wilderness.

Arriving back at Katherine's ranch without Cimarron, Rem explained, "I don't know how many other mountain lions are on that path, but there's one less now. He killed Cimarron, and he tried to get me, too. I guess it wasn't time for me to go, but it was pretty darn close."

Rem gathered his things, and said, "I'm heading home now, Katherine. Thank you for your hospitality."

"Not heading to Montana anymore?"

Rem took the claw out of his pocket and said, "No need. Anger doesn't get you anywhere, and I'm choosing to treat every day as a blessing from this day forward."

Katherine handed Rem a bag and said, "Thank you, Rem. I made ham and cheese sandwiches for your trip. I'm so sorry about Cimarron, but I'm so happy you're okay. It's fortuitous that you were able to unjam the gun in time."

Rem nodded and a slight smile inched its way onto his lips. "Yes. Fortuitous indeed."

***

Rem stopped at the rangers' station to report killing the mountain lion and describing where to find it, Rem drove on to Lyons, where he pulled over in a grocery store parking lot to eat his sandwiches and call Ted.

After Rem told Ted's secretary who was calling, Ted came on the line and said, "To what do I owe this call, since neither of us really wants to talk to the other?"

Rem replied, "If I were you, I would close the door to your office, sit down, and listen very closely. I just had a long visit with Chet's wife, Katherine. You remember Katherine, don't you? She is one of the women you raped at our fraternity house, you slimeball."

Ted fired back, "You can't prove that, and I would say the statute of limitations has run out after so many years. So let's end this call, and you can go shoot some rattlesnakes, Cowboy."

"Oh, I wouldn't hang up yet, Mr. Hotshot. Katherine has written a letter about what you did. Two of her sorority sisters, Katie and Carol, have also signed it, stating that you also raped them. Yes, the statute of limitations has passed, but they are ready to send this letter or fly to New York to inform your board of directors about your real character. Do I have your attention yet?"

In a tone that signaled resignation, Ted said, "Okay, Rem, what do you want me to do to make this all go away?"

"Here's the deal," Rem stated calmly. "I told Chet to come and meet with your assistant tomorrow to sign loan extension papers. I would like you to see that the loan is extended for another 10 years, and since the financial crisis is over, it would only be fair to reduce the interest rate by 1%. If you do that, I will make sure the women do not proceed with their plan, and I promise to never bring up the topic again. Do we have a deal?"

Ted huffed, "You are one son of a bitch, and I would love to tear you apart. But seeing that you haven't given me much of a choice…you have a deal. I will have the papers ready tomorrow for Chet to sign." That said, he ended the call. With a wide grin on his face, Rem took a big bite of his sandwich and pulled his truck and trailer back on the road to head home.

CHAPTER 21
ALIVE...BUT NOT WELL

The chemo infusion room was quiet except for the soft hum of machines and the occasional rustle of a nurse's footsteps. Callie leaned back in the recliner, her gaze fixed on the slow drip of the IV bag above her. The mastectomy was behind her now, and she was bracing herself for the battle ahead, but the stillness of these sessions gave her too much time to think. Too much time to wonder if she'd made a mistake with Rem. She missed him—the passion they'd shared, the spark of independence he'd awakened in her. She missed the version of herself she'd found when she was with him, a woman who felt free, alive, and happy. Callie sighed, her chest tightening with regret. It was too late to reclaim that life; it was gone forever. She wasn't that person now, and she didn't want Rem to see her this way.

Through the surgeries, the grueling treatments, and the slow, aching recovery, Callie carried a weight heavier than the illness itself—regret. Again and again, she took the long way home, letting familiar places pull her back to the life she might have had with Rem. Tears burned her cheeks as she whispered apologies into the empty air. But she never dared to drive out to the ranch. She knew that if she did, she would turn through the gate, drive down to the barn, step out of the car, and look into his eyes. And then she would say the words that had lived in her heart for far too long: "Hi, my name is Callie Rose Parker. Could I spend the rest of my life here?"

Resigned to live the life that she had chosen, she found that time marched by very slowly. The only thing that changed was her reflection in the mirror. Sure, she had some adventures with her girlfriends, nice outings with the grandkids, and a few small visits with her sister, but the joy she had found with Rem was pushed into a distant memory.

What kept her alive was the fact that the memories of her time with Rem were theirs alone. Only she and Rem shared those memories, so they would never be tarnished by what others might say or think. To keep her memories shiny and clear, as if they happened yesterday, she secretly pulled out her journals every so often to relive the moments she'd had with Rem. Reading about the wild horse galloping across the meadow reminded her of her first glimpse of what freedom looked like, and having Rem unwrap his dessert in the Evergreen cabin brought forth the thought that life is nothing more than a series of memories as we get older. The key to a happy life is making as many happy memories as possible.

Callie had stayed with Bill—not out of love, but out of a weary mix of duty, habit, and the quiet dread of facing her illness alone. Her marriage hadn't improved; if anything, his absence had only grown. But that didn't trouble her. What anchored her, what made staying bearable, was the warmth of her grandson and granddaughter nearby. Being a grandmother filled the hollow spaces Bill left behind, and she clung to that joy with everything she had.

Her Grandma Rose had been such a great example of how to relate to grandkids. Spending time with Grandma Rose in her garden had been one of the memorable highlights of her childhood. She could hear Grandma Rose say, "The song of the meadowlark welcomes you at the beginning of the day and says goodnight to you when the sun sets in the west. Listen closely, Rose: meadowlarks have a complex, two-phase song that begins with 1 to 6 whistles and descends to a series of 1 to 5 warbles."

Callie taught her granddaughter Anna about growing roses and listening to the song of the meadowlark. Her grandson Colton had loved cowboys and horses since he was a toddler. Since she and Bill had five acres, she convinced Bill to build a little barn and to buy Colton a black pony. Bill, feeling guilty about never being home, agreed, "Go ahead and hire a contractor to do it. Make sure they do a good job and don't cost us a fortune. Whatever you do, you should realize that the upkeep of the barn and feeding and care of the animal is going to be on you because I'm not doing it."

"I know, I know. But Colton needs to have something. He'll help sometimes. I'll teach him. You won't have to do it, Bill."

"Yeah, because you know so much about caring for horses after a part-time job shoveling shit," Bill muttered.

But Callie knew. After working for Rem, she knew how to clean stalls and looked forward to teaching Colton the same skills. She decided that they would name the pony Cimarron. Not that she needed a reason, but Callie secretly wanted to think about Rem as often as possible.

Over the next few months, Callie worked with the contractor to build a barn that would be comfortable and welcoming. She smiled as she helped the architect plan her vision. As each board was nailed to the frame, only Callie knew that it was a replica of Rem's barn, just a smaller version. It wasn't Rem, but she wanted to feel his presence. She knew Bill would never so much as set foot in the barn, so she hung a small shadow box containing two dried roses formerly hidden in the bottom drawer of the China cabinet.

Colton took to Cimarron immediately, and Cimarron reciprocated. Callie knew that the gentle pony would teach her grandson how to ride confidently as they grew up together, and Colton would learn unconditional love, loyalty, and reliance. She would teach Colton how to click commands with his tongue, and how to train Cimarron to respond in kind.

Each early morning, Callie brushed Cimarron and spoke softly, telling him about her life and love and love lost. She wasn't lonely when she was in the barn. It was home. "Cimarron, you'll never know my cowboy; his eyes were as vast as the sky, and his heart was as big and open as the whole of Douglas County." Callie pressed her hand against the pony's warm muzzle and looked into his dark brown eyes where she found peace. She whispered, "Oh, and Cimarron, his lips. They were like heaven."

CHAPTER 22
FORTUITOUS AGAIN?

As Callie left the grocery store, she remembered that she needed to stop by Home Depot to pick up a drill bit. Even though she still lived her life using the word "fortuitous" as her compass, she never felt that she had telepathy. However, ever since she woke up this morning, something had felt different. She couldn't put her finger on it, but it felt like all her senses were on high alert.

Sitting in the parking lot of Home Depot, Rem double checked his list to make sure he had remembered everything. As he was doing so, he looked over at the car that pulled in next to him. As the woman walked by his passenger window, he could swear that it was Callie. It had been a long time since he had last seen her and she looked different somehow, but he recognized the gentle curves of her face. His heart beat like crazy as he waited for her to come back. He rolled the passenger window down so he could call out her name when she returned to her car.

When he spotted her again, he shouted her name.

Callie turned toward the truck, and the moment her eyes landed on him, recognition hit. *Rem.*

A grin broke across her face, warm and familiar. "Oh my gosh, I can't believe it's you! How have you been? This is just… well, fortuitous."

Rem let out a small laugh, shaking his head. "If anyone would call this fortuitous, it's you." His voice was light, but there was something else beneath it—something quieter, almost reverent. "It's really nice to see you."

For a brief moment, he hesitated, wanting to ask her right then and there to go for coffee, to sit across from her and make up for all the lost time. But instead, he took a breath and asked, "Would you like to grab a coffee tomorrow? We could catch up."

Callie's smile softened. "I would love that. I'm actually leaving in the morning to visit my sister in Hilton Head for the next three weeks. She's the only family I have left now, since my parents are gone."

She paused, then added, "Could I call you when I get back? Fate is being this generous, so of course we should talk."

He replied, "Count on it." They continued to talk for the next few minutes, telling each other about their kids and the grandchildren. Small talk.

He thought it would only be right to tell her that he was no longer married. "Callie, I must tell you that Jane and I divorced a few years ago. My son Jack is running the ranch now. I help him out about three days a week. I am living in that little cabin in Evergreen." With a smile and mischievous twinkle in his eyes, he said, "I think you probably remember the cabin I am talking about, right?"

Caught off guard, Callie's mouth went dry, and she felt that old familiar tingle between her legs. "I do remember, and please know that I will never forget," she replied as her knees became weak. Knowing better, but with the words flowing out of her mouth, she said, "Do you live there alone, or do you... um... do you have someone?"

"I live there alone. It's my favorite place to enjoy my hobby of sculpting Western art. Well, I better quit jawboning and let you run. I look forward to that coffee when you get back. Cream only and no sugar, right?"

She tilted her head and commented, "Good memory, Cowboy."

July 21, 2003

Dear Journal,

I can't believe that I ran into Rem today. After all this time... was it fortuity/serendipity? And like the first time I met him, he took my breath away just looking at him. He's still so incredibly handsome, and now, with that salt and pepper hair--it just adds to his raw sexiness. Between that and all the talk about our time together in the Evergreen cabin, I was worried I was going to have a car accident on the way home. My mind was definitely wandering.

It's hard to believe that he's been single for years and no one has snatched him up yet. How is that even possible? I'll have to ask him about that when we meet for coffee. He also needs to know why I left and stayed away. I will tell him about my breast cancer. I owe him that.

CHAPTER 23
WEEKS WENT BY

After talking with Callie, Rem found himself drawn more and more to the ranch, a place chock-full of memories, good and bad. He spent more and more of his time there, helping his son mend all the smooth wire fencing in the different pastures and around the ranch's perimeter. Not only did he volunteer to take on this chore, but he felt closer to his memories of Callie when he was working at the ranch. It also gave him an opportunity to train his new horse to be a true ranch horse. He missed Cimarron. They'd had a bond that would be indescribable to a person who had never experienced sharing friendship and trust with an animal.

A true ranch horse is trained differently from other saddle horses. You first teach them to react to voice commands instead of only using the reins. One click of the tongue means to walk on, two clicks to trot, and three clicks to explode with a gallop. This allows for faster action when working with a herd of horses or cattle.

Rem liked to use a hackamore bridle since his new horse did not like a metal bit in its mouth. He felt the horse could graze better while he was off fixing the fence. A true ranch horse was also taught to stand in one area when the rider dismounted. This was better than head-tying him to a fence post or tree. One other talent Rem liked to add was to train the horse to come to him when he whistled.

As Rem tightened the top wire, he glanced toward the ranch gate and spotted a FedEx truck making its way down to the barn. Curious, he set his tools aside and whistled for his new horse, Shawnee. The horse trotted over, and Rem swung into the saddle, clicking his tongue three times. Shawnee broke into a gallop, carrying him swiftly toward the barn to see what was being delivered. Maybe it was something that required his signature. A thought flickered through his mind—could it be something from Callie?

After signing the FedEx envelope, he tore it open and saw it was from The Ministry of Defence in London, England. They were presenting his dad with an award for all the flights he had flown for England during WWII. Since it would be awarded posthumously, they wanted to know if Rem was available to travel to London to accept the award on behalf of his father.

Feeling honored and proud of his dad, he sent back his acceptance the very next day. Since he had to fly into New

York from Denver to connect to his flight to London, he called Ted.

Rem then booked a room at the DoubleTree by Hilton in Manhattan. Ted said he would get dinner reservations for them just down the street.

While Rem was in New York City, he thought he would rent a car and drive to Connecticut the next day to see Jane and their younger son David, who stayed with her for part of the summer. Rem had not seen Jane since the divorce, and he thought it was time he did so. Since their divorce had not been contentious, he could never quite figure out what had kept them apart all these years.

Later that day, he let his son Jack and ranch foreman Caleb know that he would be leaving in a couple of days to attend the ceremony in London honoring Jack's grandpa.

After booking his flight to New York, he booked his flight to London. Since he had decided to drive to Connecticut to see Jane and their son David the day after he landed in New York, he booked the red-eye flight to London the next night, figuring he could sleep most of the way.

He arrived at the DoubleTree just before dinner after suffering through a slow taxi ride from JFK. He checked in, went to his room and took a shower. Then he watched the news on TV until Ted called him from the lobby.

As they left the hotel, Rem looked over at Ted and said, "Thanks for meeting me, Ted. It has been quite some time since we have spoken and a very long time since we have seen each other. Congrats on your promotion to bank president. With Wall Street just around the corner, that must put you in some mighty high circles."

"It does, Rem, and I love New York City as much as you love your ranch. I guess we both ended up where we were supposed to be," Ted said as they were seated in the restaurant. It had been quite some time since Rem had been in a restaurant with oak walls, white tablecloths, and a wine steward.

Rem raised his wine glass and said, "Life is a constant journey of self-discovery and evolution. To survive, a person has to let go of the past. It is part of moving forward. There is no way to know what makes one thing happen and not another. What leads to what? What causes what to flourish, die, or to take a different course? I salute you, my friend." He continued, "You won't believe this, but I am driving out to Bridgeport tomorrow to see Jane and my son David. It has been years since I last saw her. I'm still unsure why she hasn't wanted to stay in contact. We spent 23 years together, and we have two sons."

Ted looked at Rem and said, "Rem, Jane has asked me to request that you don't go to Bridgeport to see her tomorrow."

"And you know this how?"

Ted hesitated, "I guess I also need to let you know that Jane and I are engaged and have been seeing each other for some time. She feels it would be quite awkward."

"Well, my friend," Rem replied, "That is quite a revelation. I can't figure out why it was kept from me until now. I don't have any feelings for her, but I am confused about why you do. Back in college, you described her as a stuck-up bitch who only thought of herself. You kept telling me not to get engaged to her. You continually warned me that she would make a terrible wife. When I think about it, I wonder if you like her or her father more." Ted furrowed his brow angrily as he blurted out, "Why would you say that? You have spent too much time in the hot sun being a cowboy…a stupid cowboy at that."

Rem narrowed his gaze and locked eyes with Ted, delivering an answer that made fear flicker across Ted's face. "When you told me that you were appointed bank president, I went on the Internet to do some research about the bank and its clients. It didn't surprise me to find out that Jane's father's hedge fund company was the bank's largest client. At the time, I thought nothing of it. Now I get the picture. New York City has changed you from who you used to be, Ted. And I might add that it's not for the better. I'm sure it has crossed your mind what your career path will be when you are no longer bank president. I have a sneaky suspicion that you are planning to be the president of a large hedge fund. Yes, I know that you think I am just a stupid cowboy. However, out west, we have a term for city slickers like you: scoundrel. In the Old West, they used to hang them up from the nearest tree. Now we just look down on them. I guess I would rather be hanged than be looked down upon."

Standing up, Rem continued, "Well, enjoy your dinner alone. Don't worry, I won't mention anything to Jane about all the terrible things you used to say about her. I also won't tell her about your hedge fund plan for the future. She doesn't deserve to have that on her mind. Yes, I could be wrong about the hedge fund plan, but I will keep tabs on you on the Internet over the next couple of years just in case you don't send me an announcement. I hope you don't have plans to come to Douglas County, Colorado, because I know the perfect tree to string you up from. Thanks for the wine."

Furious, Ted slid his chair back and stood up. After Rem shot him a "Don't try me" look, he sat back down.

Walking out of the restaurant, Rem called the Hilton on his cell phone. He requested they call British Airways to see if he could move his red eye flight to tonight instead of waiting a day.

When he arrived at the Hilton, the concierge confirmed the new flight time. The hotel would have a shuttle ready to go to JFK in one hour. As he packed his bags, his thoughts turned to Callie and how much he missed her.

Making his way down the aisle of the Boeing 777, he spotted his seat. In the same row was a very attractive woman with her book already opened for the long trip ahead.

Rem introduced himself to her after placing his briefcase in the upper bin. He learned her name was Andrea and that she was flying to London to see her husband perform in a stage play at the Adelphi Theater. Her husband usually performed in New York City, but his stage company had a booking in London for the next two months.

Once Rem was settled in his seat, Andrea looked over and said, "So, Rem Cunningham, as you get to know me, you will find that I am always full of questions. First of all, is Rem your real name? Secondly, I have to ask what you do, where you are from, and why are you going to London?"

Rem replied, "My real name is Remington. Secondly, look down at my boots, and you will figure it out…Sorry, it's not funny. Andrea, I am from Colorado, and I am a rancher. I'm flying to London to accept a posthumous award for my father, who was a pilot who flew out of England in WWII. Again, I'm sorry I was so rude telling you to look at my cowboy boots to get your answer. The last few hours have been quite stressful, and I don't think I have wrapped my arms around what just happened."

Smiling, she said, "Remington…sorry, Rem, today is your lucky day. I am a psychologist and would be happy to talk about your day if you need to."

With a twinkle in her eyes and a big smile, she added, "With you being a cowboy and me loving stories about the Old West, my hourly rate will be $0 as long as you tell me about your ranch and horses."

Rem said with a wink, "You have a deal, Andrea. I'm not sure you want to hear about what happened today, but I would love to tell you about my ranch and horses."

Rem found that talking to Andrea came easily. He told her about Ted and what he had learned at dinner.

She concurred with his analysis of what was really taking place. There was no doubt in her mind that Ted wanted to be the president of the Livingston Hedge Fund and that Jane was just part of the package.

Andrea knew first hand what it was like to be a part of a package. "I feel more like baggage these days. Not much like part of a package in my marriage these days."

Rem said, "Sorry. Too bad we don't know a therapist or psychologist or something."

"True, true. That would be nice," she laughed.

They both decided to get some sleep since it was such a long flight. After about three hours of dozing, Andrea woke up and saw that Rem was already awake. In the dimly lit cabin of the plane, it appeared that a tear was slowly descending down his cheek. She touched his forearm, which rested on the armrest, and said, "Rem, is everything okay? I will shut up and leave you alone if you prefer. Just let me know if you want to talk."

He looked over at her and saw that she really meant what she was saying. Deciding to open up about his situation with Callie, he said, "Andrea, what happened with Ted isn't really what is troubling me. Just recently, I reconnected with the love of my life. Since I've described her to you as the love of my life, you are probably picturing a romantic encounter. I must tell you that it took place in a Home Depot parking lot. "After we parted ways years ago, I had not seen her at all until just a couple of weeks ago. Talking to her for just a few minutes reminded me that

I love her as much now as I did then. She ended our relationship years ago because she felt she had an obligation to her family. I could understand her convictions, but at the same time, I knew she loved me more than life itself. After we visited for a while, she agreed to have coffee with me when she gets back from a vacation in Hilton Head."

He went on to say, "So, Miss Psychologist, when I see her next, should I go after her with abandon and maybe be subjected to pain again, or should I just protect myself by saying hi and then go down the road with fond memories?"

Andrea shifted in her seat to look directly at him. "Before I can objectively talk to you and maybe provide you with some good advice, I need to confess something. I say 'confess' because it would be unethical for me to advise you when I have been trying to come up with the same answer you are looking for. The reason I am flying to London is to ask my husband for a divorce. Before I say more, let me quote my favorite philosopher, Joseph Campbell: 'Sometimes we should give up the life we planned so that we can have the life that is waiting for us.'

"Rem, I know there is a life waiting for me that includes those feelings of love that you have for Callie. I want nothing less, so I'm willing to move on since I don't have those feelings of love for my husband. Maybe I will lose, or perhaps I will win. That said, my advice to you is that it all boils down to making a decision…nothing more and nothing less. I do know you already have her heart."

Rem asked, "I still don't understand life well enough to figure out what to do. Should we have stayed together back then and lived life like we wanted it to be? Should we have parted ways like we did so that other people would not be hurt? Is it right to leave a person you really love and end up with years of sadness? Will the same questions be facing us again 10 years from now? Do we have to make the same decisions we faced before? So, Andrea, with that many questions, are you sure you want to keep your rate at $0?"

"Rem, I'm glad I told you about my marriage difficulties because I can identify with you. I could say that I also need a psychologist to answer those questions, but these questions don't deal with psychological problems. They deal with life decisions based on heartfelt emotions. We sometimes refer to these as psychosocial problems. With that being said, I cannot advise you on any certain course of action. You have a decision to make, and that is all there is to it. I know that because I have struggled with mine for months, with many sleepless nights and tears on my pillow."

After a few more hours of sleep, their plane touched down at Heathrow Airport. Rem and Andrea gave each other a goodbye hug. Rem leaned in close and said, "Thank you so much for telling me your story about a future life that might be waiting for both of us. I will follow your advice. I decided while I slept that I wanted to get Callie back. Without her, I don't feel like I have a life. Let me know if you ever make it to Colorado. Callie and I will take you for a beautiful early evening horseback ride."

CHAPTER 24
AND TIME SLIPS AWAY

Throughout her vacation in Hilton Head, Callie's thoughts kept returning to her fortuitous meeting with Rem at the hardware store. Seeing Rem's face and hearing his voice had given her the same joy and anticipation she had felt on Christmas morning as a child. The excitement was overwhelming.

What was she going to do and say when they were together again? She still loved Rem more than anything else in life. But even though her parents were gone and her sons were adults, she now had grandchildren to consider…a new responsibility.

As Callie sat in a sailboat off the shore of Hilton Head one evening at sunset, she closed her eyes as memories of her adventures with Rem filled her mind. She remembered the horseback ride they had taken along Plum Creek and the romantic moments they'd shared at the cabin in Evergreen. More than anything, she recalled how Rem had always taken care of her and made her feel so beautiful even when she was sweaty from mucking out stalls.

Over the past several years her life had been pleasant, but deep inside, she felt lonely. She yearned for that loving feeling she had experienced all those years ago. She longed for the sense of freedom she had discovered. And most of all, she missed being the Callie that had come alive when she was with Rem. She missed the real Callie, the Callie who was authentically and truly herself. If she had a dollar for every night that she fell asleep with tears on her pillow, she would be a very wealthy woman.

As the sun dipped lower in the sky, the idea of Rem being a newly single man and living alone lingered in her thoughts. She pictured him living in the cabin and imagined how he would have decorated it with Western artifacts. She thought about the wild rose bushes along the front porch. Adjacent to the two sofas would be a large, comfortable leather chair where he would spend his time reading. She remembered the log frame bed with the Canadian red-and-black plaid wool blanket. What added to the craziness in her brain was how she pictured herself there. She imagined taking afternoon walks with Rem, cooking dinner together, and relaxing on the rug in front of the fireplace. She was brought back to reality when a wave hit the side of the boat and sprayed her with cold water.

She and Beth returned to the dock. As she relished the sounds of the seagulls and the smell of ocean air, she felt melancholy but excited at the same time. Tomorrow she would be on her way home.

August 10, 2003

Dear Journal,

 I am really struggling with what I should say and do when I see Rem. I am so nervous, but at the same time I have never been so eager to see someone's face and hear their voice. I've missed having him in my life. Should I give him my goodbye letter, or should I give him my heart and soul? My tears are staining this page with the struggle I am feeling in my heart.

 I can't bear the thought of giving him the goodbye letter and seeing the grief in his eyes. I have never faced anything so hard in my life. After weeks of soul searching, do I put love of family first or my love for this man first?

August 10, 2003

My Dearest Rem,

Even though I know I love you with all my heart, I feel compelled to write you this letter. My love for you is timeless. It is as strong today as the day I fell in love with you. Yet my love of family is deep, and my obligations are a commitment woven deep down in my soul.

How hard it is for me to give up my hopes for what the future could bring. I do have and will treasure the memory of all the events we shared. I feel most grateful to you for giving me those memories.

Never forget how much I loved you.
Callie

August 10, 2003

Hey Cowboy,

For two weeks, I've cried tears of sadness and tears of joy. The memories of all the moments we spent together come crowding over me as I write to you. I feel grateful to God that you entered my life. You may not know it, but my life is now centered on what you taught me and how much you loved me... a love I have never felt before or since.

If you still need a stable hand and someone to ride double with, I would like to come back to work at the ranch forever and ever.

I can't wait for you to hold me and for me to look into those eyes that set me on fire. I've waited 7 years for you to make love to me, and I can't wait another week.

Callie

CHAPTER 25
NO...THAT CAN'T BE

Callie felt as giddy as a schoolgirl as she prepared for her return trip to Colorado. She was eager to see Rem's piercing but warm, inviting eyes peering over his cup of coffee as he looked at her. The way he stared at her was like having foreplay. No man had ever looked at her that way. His eyes always had a way of making her melt. At the same time, she was feeling lost and uncertain about the future.

She heard her sister Beth calling the airport shuttle to arrange a ride to the Hilton Head Airport in Savannah. As she packed her suitcases, she wondered what life would bring when she got home. She still had no idea what she was going to do. No instant answer came to her mind.

Callie had placed her journal and some other personal items in a safe deposit box at her sister's bank. She'd given Beth a key to the box with instructions about what to do if anything ever happened to her. She remembered looking directly at her sister and saying, "Sis, if I've learned nothing else in life, it's my own mortality. I put some stuff in a safe deposit box at the bank. If you ever need to retrieve my things, there's a journal. Please give me your word that you will won't read it. It contains a part of my soul. I only want to share it with one person. A person who owned my heart. I will share my secret with you, but the words in my journal are only for him."

Callie told Beth the story of what happened seven years ago and how she and Rem had met again recently. "Beth, he made me so happy. It was just not to be, given my circumstances. I didn't want to burden him with my treatment and all that. When I get home, I'm going to have coffee with him and catch up. Who knows."

The sisters hugged and talked about Callie's options, and speaking softly and tearfully, Beth said, "Callie, I want to tell you my thoughts, but I respect that this is your decision. Sis, a love like this rarely comes along in life. Ever since we were little girls and throughout life, you have always put everyone else first. Then you were finally able to experience true freedom and to be in touch with your spirit. Did God will this to happen? Was it fortuitous or just plain old destiny? I don't know, but it happened. When you talk about Rem, your eyes and voice enter another world."

On the ride to the airport on Highway 278, Callie stared out the window of the shuttle at the forest next to the road. If only life were as simple and peaceful as the

Southern Live Oak trees with the Spanish moss draped on their limbs.

Callie reached for her purse on the seat next to her and pulled out the two letters. One letter said goodbye to Rem, and the other declared herself eternally his for life. With her decision now clear, she needed to discard the letter contradicting her choice. She didn't want to litter, but in a decisive moment, she slightly lowered the window and let the unwanted letter flutter away. This simple act, breaking from her usual principles, surprisingly eased a burden from her shoulders, flooding her with relief.

As the shuttle approached the Bluffton turnoff and entered Highway 46, her eyes locked on a car as it barreled through the intersection in slow motion. Instantly, the car slammed into the left side of the shuttle, throwing it onto its side and shattering her moment of clarity and bliss.

Callie could hear someone calling 911. In the ambulance on the way to the hospital she remembered that she had told Rem when they parted years ago, "Before I die, I wanted to know what it is like to love a man truly…and now I do."

Going in and out of consciousness, Callie thought about Rem's favorite Garth Brooks song, *If Tomorrow Never Comes*. Rem had told her, "Callie, this isn't exactly how Garth sang the song, but I want to tell you my version, okay?

Sometimes late at night,
I turn out the lights and pretend you're sleeping next to me.
And the thought crosses my mind:
How would I feel if you didn't wake up in the morning?
If your life on earth were through,
Would you know how much I loved you?
If tomorrow never comes,
Would you know you were my only one?

Callie closed her eyes as she mouthed the words, smiled, and took her final breath, uttering his name, "Rem."

CHAPTER 26
JUST CAN'T WAIT

With a load of hay on his flatbed trailer, Rem listened to oldie country tunes on his radio. Some of the songs had a special meaning from his time with Callie—they made him ache and smile. He could not wait to call her, since he knew she had just returned from spending three weeks at Hilton Head. *Had it only been three?*

After their chance meeting at Home Depot, she agreed to join him for a cup of coffee. He planned to get it to go and take her for a ride—just like old times. He'd spent countless early mornings retracing their route alone, longing for the quiet intimacy they once shared over coffee and open roads.

He had already made plans for their reunion ride. First, he rehearsed what he wanted to tell Callie. The most important thing to say to her was how she had been an angel lifting him up and coaching him through his difficult financial crisis with his brother. He owed her a big thank you for that. These thoughts had been on his mind for so many long years. He needed to give her that big thank you. He had always regretted that he had not thanked her on the last day they had spent together.

Just in case this would be their only meeting, he bought her a beautiful gold angel necklace for her to have forever. He spent days going to stores looking for just the right one. If she consented to see him again, he planned to share the bottle of wine she'd brought him from France years ago. He had stared at that bottle many times through the years, imagining about how exciting it would be if they could finally share it. He just knew they would share it someday. And, of course, he would have her favorite flower, a rose, waiting for her.

Who knows? Maybe this would be what they call a second chance. A second chance at love. A second chance at life. However, a second chance was not his main purpose for the meeting. It was to give his angel the thank you she deserved. Or was that the main reason?

Since it was close to lunchtime, he decided to stop at an old rustic place where they used to eat lunch when she worked at the ranch. Every time they had lunch together, it had made the day feel complete. He was hoping today's special was Mexican enchiladas, her favorite.

Sitting down at the counter, he glanced around and noticed his insurance agent having lunch with a client. As Rem settled onto the stool, their eyes met. The agent hesitated, then slowly stood, his expression unreadable. He walked over, hesitating for just a second before speaking. He said, "Rem, did you hear about Callie…the gal who used to work for you a while back? I heard that she died in a car accident just outside Savannah. Shuttle bus got T-boned or something. I heard she died in the ambulance on the way to the hospital. Darn shame. Nice gal."

Rem's mind went numb. For a moment, he couldn't speak. He swallowed hard, forcing himself to respond. "Oh… I didn't know." His voice came out flat, almost robotic. "Uh, thanks for letting me know." A pause, too long. He needed to get out of there. "I just remembered—I'm supposed to pick up my grandson from school. Sorry, I've gotta run."

He rushed out of the restaurant and barely made it to his truck before the dam burst. As soon as he got into the driver's seat, the tears started to flow down his face. He immediately started the engine and drove away as fast as he could. Less than a mile down the road, he had to pull over. Laying his forehead on the steering wheel, he sobbed like he had never cried before. His body trembled and shook with grief. When he started his truck again, he drove to Callie's favorite jogging road.

Not a soul had known about their past relationship. He could not share his grief with anyone. He also could not talk with mutual friends to confirm the details of what had happened. If he tried to get more information, he knew he would break down on the spot when they mentioned her name and said that it was true. In the back of his mind he was clinging to the possibility that it wasn't true. It just couldn't be true. Not with the plans that he had already made for their next meeting.

CHAPTER 27
SAY GOODBYE

Days passed before Rem finally mustered up the courage to look online at the obituaries for the local funeral home. He wanted to believe that Callie was still alive. When he saw her obituary and picture, he felt like his heart had been torn out of his chest. Yes, she had died. Now he had to admit it and face it.

Staying away from her funeral was beyond heartbreaking. He needed to be there for her. He needed to say goodbye. However, he knew that he would not be able to make it through the service without breaking down. Too many people would notice his reaction. During the funeral, he sat in his truck parked near the church. Throngs of people attended the service, showing how much she had meant to the community. Rem's tears would not stop flowing, his whole body shaking with uncontrollable sobbing as he realized Callie was gone forever.

After seeing everyone leave the church, he drove home with the knowledge that he had entered a different world where he would no longer have her love. Different from when a person is younger, some of the changes that occur when you are older result in two final labels: "Gone" and "Never Again."

He put one of Callie's favorite Garth Brooks CDs in the player and listened to "The Dance."

When they'd parted ways seven years ago, Callie had tucked a note between the seat cushions as she jumped out of the pickup truck. He had read it and re-read it so many times that he could quote it from memory:

Rem,

I am sure that Garth had us in mind when he wrote "The Dance."

Like the song said, "Before meeting you, never in my life did I feel the world was right."

The Dance we shared allowed me to feel freedom and romantic love for the first time. I would have never guessed that it would be me who said goodbye. You were my everything, and you will always be. The pain I feel is beyond words, but I replace the pain every day, knowing that I did not miss the Dance.

Thank you, Cowboy!

CHAPTER 28
MY SOUL HAS BEEN SET FREE

Rem went through the motions of living despite the pain, loneliness, and anger bottled up inside. Now that Callie was gone forever, he would never get the chance to tell her how he felt about her. Never again whisper in her ear. Never again squeeze her hand. He constantly thought about how she had always been there when he was upset. He would look over and admire her beautiful face and kind smile. Those wide blue eyes would look at him with adoration and love. She had so much understanding of what a man was all about and needed. And she was so beautiful. There had never been an unpleasant word between them. They'd just laughed, played, talked, and looked at the beautiful Douglas County scenery.

Without saying a word, she had provided the affirmation his ego had needed. Rem remembered saying to her,

"You are like an angel of mercy that was sent to me out of the sky when I was in desperate need. Where in the world did you come from? How can you be so different? Why do you bother to care for me?" She didn't have angel wings then. Now, both Megan and Callie had donned their very own angel wings.

Rem knew that part of his pain came from not being able to share his story with anyone. He had no one to grieve with. Their relationship had to remain private, like it had remained all these years.

A month after Callie died, Rem received a FedEx package from Callie's sister Beth in Hilton Head. Opening the box, he saw a journal with a note taped to the front of it. The handwritten note was from Callie's sister. She wrote, "Callie brought her journal when she came to see me. While she was here, she rented a safe deposit box at my bank. She gave me a key and a sealed envelope that said to only open it upon her death and follow the instructions inside. We both laughed and acknowledged that it would be way down the road. After I received the call that she died, I went to the bank and opened the safe deposit box. Returning home, I opened the envelope and followed the instructions telling me to send the diary to you. The note said that I should never mention to anyone that she had a journal nor that I had sent it to you. She also begged me not to read the journal before sending it to you. Just so you know, as her sister and best friend, I did not read it.

"Before I end this letter, let me say that she was such a special and unique person. I have loved her with all my heart since we were little girls. I have tears in my eyes thinking of what you must have meant to her. Thank you for taking care of my little Sis. I know she must have truly loved you to give you this private treasure."

He held the journal close to his heart as he walked over to his favorite leather chair in the cabin. He was in utter disbelief that he was holding Callie's personal journal. It was so much like her to think of doing this for him. Not yet prepared to open it, he headed to the kitchen to get a cup of coffee.

As he opened the journal, he felt like she was sitting there in the cabin with him. He would always hold her in his heart, but now he was holding a piece of her. He spent the next five hours reading and re-reading her journal entries. She had such a beautiful way with words; she was so tender and loving. When he read the entries where she was struggling and sad, he just wanted to wrap her in his arms and never let go.

"Callie, I don't know how this works, but just know you will never, ever be alone again."

Before finishing the journals, Rem put his head back in the leather chair to rest his eyes. Without falling asleep, he opened his eyes and saw Callie standing in front of the arm of his chair. Not knowing what to do, he stared at her like she was a vision, not a dream.

Gazing back at him, Callie whispered, "Don't weep for me! Don't be sad! My soul has been set free! Do not grieve for me because I will be right there in everything you love. I'll be in the morning sun! I will be in the Colorado blue sky! I will be in the smell of wild roses in the spring and the pine needles in the fall! I will be with you when you are riding a galloping horse. Most of all, my dearest Rem, I will be with you in all your dreams."

Before he could respond, she was gone. Had it been a vision, or was it a dream? Thinking about it, he knew Callie had just come to him in a vision…she had been right there before him.

Rem went to his bedroom and tucked the journal under his pillow, then grabbed his hat and left the cabin.

He walked along his favorite path and thought about the treasure he had been given. Even though he knew Callie was gone, it felt like she was there, walking and lying next to him—such a comfort.

Needing to sign some legal papers on ranch business, he called his attorney to schedule a time to meet. The paralegal, Maria, answered the phone and said the documents were all typed and ready to be signed. Maria said she was making a trip to the courthouse in Douglas County. She volunteered to bring the papers with her and give them to him. He suggested lunch if that worked for her.

He'd had lunch with her before and enjoyed her company. Although she was matronly in appearance, her personality was always very bubbly and happy. Rem always greeted her in the office with, "Hey, my little girl from Mexico." She had migrated to the U.S. about 40 years earlier at age 16. He really enjoyed that she still had a little accent that made her voice so captivating. She spoke very softly with a cadence that reminded him of how Callie had spoken. Not knowing what came over him at lunch, he said, "I really need to talk to you. I am picking you to talk to because I trust you and you shared your tragic, sad story with me a year ago. However, I need you to agree to full confidentiality. Let me first say, during the time you have worked for Jim, I have seen so much depth in your demeanor. I am so impressed with how you have handled your life. Is it all right for me to tell you what's on my mind?"

She nodded, "Please, of course, and thank you for the kind words. I have been impressed with who you are since you first walked into Jim's office. I will never forget what you did for my son to get him into the Air Force Academy. He is now a fighter pilot. He and I both know that you assisted in giving him a life he is proud of."

Telling her the story about Callie was very difficult, but he could feel a sense of relief start to come over him. However, he broke down in tears when he told her what had happened a month ago. He told her the last words Callie had said to him seven years ago when they'd parted ways.

"Maria, Callie leaned in, looked directly into my eyes, and said, 'All my life, I have wondered what it would be like to love a man before I die. And now I know. Thank you for making my dream come true.'"

Maria could see the sadness in his face and feel the pain in his heart. After listening to his story, she had shed tears of her own. He looked at her and said, "I just can't believe it is over forever and ever. I will no longer have that connection and love in my life. Even though the love and connection had been from afar for so long, I knew she was somewhere nearby. It felt so good to know she was nearby, but now she is gone."

He took a deep breath and then continued talking. "Not knowing if you believe in the afterlife or that people can cross over in the form of a vision, I need to tell you what happened last night."

"Marie, Callie came to me last night as I sat in my big old leather chair. She stood right in front of me and said she would always be riding alongside me. She said she is in the smell of wild roses in the spring and the pine needles in the fall. She told me not to weep for her."

Maria's voice, in her beautiful accent, said, "Rem, I do believe in visions from people who have passed over to the afterlife. You do have Callie's love in your life. She is gone from this earth but not from your heart. And this isn't one-sided, Rem. Please look at me and never forget what I am going to tell you. Right at this moment, she is still loving you, even though she is not here with you."

Rem looked at her and said, "Maria, your beautiful words have made me so happy. I know that I will never stop loving her, but I never thought she could still love me forever, even though she told me she would in my vision. This is the first moment that I have felt contentment and acceptance."

With those words, a feeling of joy went through his entire body that lifted the weight off his shoulders, allowing him to sit up straighter in the booth. It had finally crossed his mind that Callie still loved him. That thought made him smile like he had not done in months.

As he drove back to the ranch, he said to himself, "Now that I think about it, life is like a book. Each chapter takes us to the next chapter. When the chapters are all connected, as in life, a story is told. We are kept in suspense about how the book is going to end until we reach the final chapter."

Arriving back at the ranch, he walked into the barn and went to the tack room to get his saddle. He needed to take a long ride on Shawnee to clear his mind. Sliding open the door, he saw a rose lying on his saddle. He knew it had to be the rose that Callie Rose had put on the shelf above the saddle rack years earlier. It must have blown down, but he couldn't help but think that Callie had put it there to remind him that she would be with him forever.

CHAPTER 29
...AND LIFE WENT ON

Over the next year, Rem kept to himself. He had lost his brother and his parents to death, Jane to divorce, and now Callie. But why? During the day, he did chores and worked on training young horses. That had once been the highlight of his day, but now the joy wasn't there, and it had just become a routine that got him through until it was time for supper.

Nights on the ranch seemed cold and lonely. The thought of inviting someone new into his heart and home had crossed his mind, but he couldn't shake the feeling of unease that came with it. Even though a number of women frequented the ranch and checked on the training of their horses, he wasn't interested in dating. Some of the women were so bold with their intentions that he had to ask them to trailer up their horses and take a one-way trip out of the gate.

Every evening after supper, he would sit in his big leather chair by the fireplace and read philosophy books he'd picked up at the Castle Rock public library. He read books by philosophers such as Joseph Campbell and James Allen to understand his emotions and answer all the "why's" that came with trying to make sense of what had happened to him over the last few years.

One night, he picked up Callie's journal, which he kept on his bed stand, and re-read sections that he had read a hundred times already. He kept searching for clues to what Callie was thinking and planning to do when she arrived back in Colorado. Finally, he decided to call Callie's sister Beth to ask her some questions.

The next morning, he made the call and said, "Beth, this is Rem Cunningham in Colorado. I hope I am not disturbing you, but if you have a minute? I have a couple of questions to ask you."

"Oh, hi, Rem, it is great to hear from you. Guess what," she continued. "I am packing my suitcase as we speak, since I'm flying out to Colorado to visit Callie's kids and grandchildren. I was planning to call you when I got there since I have something to give you. I would love to have dinner with you, but as you know, no one in the family can know, so I think it would be best if we met somewhere. I will tell them that I'm going to see an old college friend in Colorado Springs."

Rem replied with surprise and a lift in his voice, "That would be wonderful. With the questions I have for you, asking you in person would make all the difference in the world to me. Could we meet in Sedalia at Gabriel's restaurant at 7:00? What day works best for you?"

"Let's do it this coming Thursday; that time and location sound perfect," Beth replied. "I am so looking forward to meeting you. I feel like I know you already. See you in two days. Bye."

After saying goodbye, Rem sat in his chair and thanked God for making this happen. He was so giddy that he pulled on his boots and headed to the barn with a smile that had not been on his face for a very long time.

When Thursday evening arrived, Rem jumped into his pickup and headed to Sedalia. He wanted to be there early to greet Beth at the door of the restaurant. As she approached, looking so much like Callie, he felt a tear forming in his eye. Wiping it away, he opened the door and said, "Hi, Beth. I'm Rem."

Beth smiled, "Hi, Rem, I'm so pleased to meet you at last. Callie told me about you before she died. This timing of us needing to see each other has to be destiny in the making."

They sat and ordered a bottle of Chardonnay, and they both smiled and said at the same time, "We know Chardonnay was Callie's favorite."

"Rem, I know you said you had questions for me, but if it is okay, I would like to go first," Beth said before taking a sip of wine.

"Returning home after Callie's funeral, I started looking through things the coroner's office had boxed up and mailed to my home. They had to hold on to these things for some time because of the police investigation that took place after the accident. In her purse, I found this letter addressed to you. For some reason, thinking it didn't make a difference, I tucked it away and just recently came across it. I have to tell you that I read it, and after doing so, decided that I owe it to both Callie and you to give you the letter. I apologize for the length of time it has taken."

With that, Beth slid the letter across the table to Rem.

With an unsteady hand, Rem took the one-page letter and said, "Beth, do you mind if I read it right now? I don't think I can wait."

"Please do, and take your time. Just pour me another glass of wine first, Cowboy," Beth replied.

Rem started reading…

August 10, 2003

Hey Cowboy,

For two weeks, I've cried tears of sadness and tears of joy.

The memories of all the moments we spent together come crowding over me as I write to you. I feel grateful to God that you entered my life. You may not know it, but my life is now centered on what you taught me and how much you loved me...a love I have never felt before or since.

If you still need a stable hand and someone to ride double with, I would like to come back to the ranch forever and ever.

I can't wait for you to hold me and for me to look into those eyes that set me on fire. I've waited years for you to make love to me, and I can't wait another week.

Callie

Rem set the letter on the table and laid his hand on top of it. He stood and walked to the window, looking out to the mountains in the distance for a long moment. Beth watched him as he processed what he had read, dabbing her eyes from the streaming tears.

Rem sat back down and took Beth's hand. "Beth, what you brought me was more than a letter from Callie. It was closure, and it answered all the questions I planned to ask you this evening. I can never repay you for the kindness you've shown me. Knowing that Callie picked me to be with for the rest of her life has lifted a weight off my chest where, for the first time, I feel happiness flowing through my body. Thank you so much."

Beth whispered, "Rem, I feel Callie sitting here with us and beaming now that you know her decision to spend the rest of her life with you. Now, I want to tell you one more thing. I know my sister would be disappointed with me if I did not say this. It is time for you to be happy and move ahead with your life. She would be so sad if you lamented what happened and did not find a path forward. Knowing her as you did, you know I'm right."

Still holding Beth's hand, Rem said with strength in his voice, "I can and will do that, knowing she would be so disappointed if I did not. The treasures I have in my heart and the letter to go with her diaries will always be a part of my life and will never fade. How lucky I was to know her for such a short time." He plucked the rose from the bud vase at the end of the table. "Better take this too. I'm sure they won't mind."

After walking Beth to her car, Rem opened the door to his pickup and stared at the seat, thinking of the last time Callie had snuggled up to him. Instead of feeling despair, he smiled and made her a silent promise that he would move on with his life.

CHAPTER 30
A SURPRISE IN LIFE

About six months had passed since Rem had met with Beth in Sedalia. He'd reread Callie's letter many times, each time with a smile instead of the grief he had experienced when reading her journals. Beth had been so right when she told him that Callie would want him to move on and have happiness in his life.

As he finished his chores of watering and feeding the horses, his cell phone rang. He took the call even though he did not recognize the phone number.

"Hello, this is Rem Cunningham." Silence.

Speaking a little more loudly, he said, "This is Rem Cunningham. Can I help you?"

"Rem, this is Andrea. Do you remember me? We flew to London together when you were going to receive an award in memory of your father," she added, "I'm in Denver at a conference, and I was hoping that invitation is still open to come out and see your ranch…and hopefully to meet Callie."

Rem replied, "Andrea, of course I remember you. How great to hear from my inflight psychologist."

Taking a deep breath, Rem said with a quaver in his voice, "Andrea, Callie was killed in an auto accident on the East Coast. I'm just starting to recover from the whole ordeal. But let me stop there. We can talk further when I see you. I would love to show you the ranch and take you for that evening horseback ride I promised. When are you available?"

Andrea quietly said, "Rem, I'm so sorry, and I don't even know what to say. My heart is broken for you. I'm available to drive out Thursday afternoon. Would that work for you? If not, I understand."

"Andrea, I really would like to see you, so I will text you directions as soon as we hang up."

"Rem, again, I am so sorry but very anxious to see you again. I will look forward to your text," Andrea said.

★

Rem heard a car rumbling down the dirt road and looked toward the gate of the ranch. Andrea was driving slowly, stopping at the fork in the road. Rem stepped out of the barn and waved to her with his cowboy hat.

"Andrea, it is so good to see you again. Thank you for coming out here. It's been so… quiet. And the ranch seems so much bigger, and at the same time, smaller."

Rem held back his tears.

Andrea said, "You had a love that most people only dream about. Keep those beautiful memories front and center, since life is all about our memories."

With a smile, Rem said, "Andrea, good or bad, our lives are made up of a series of memories going all the way back to childhood. We are our memories. We can even remember the smells from our childhood. Let me be philosophical for just a minute and then we will go saddle up two horses and go for a ride. I think Michelangelo said it best: 'Men wrongly bewail the flight of time, charging that it passes too swiftly, but they fail to note that they have ample time at their disposal; for a good memory, which nature has endowed us, which makes it possible for everything that happened long ago to appear to us in the present.'

"I think you can see that I have spent too many evenings alone reading philosophers from Michelangelo to James Allen and Joseph Campbell."

Leaning in with a smile Rem added, "Now, city girl, let's head into the barn and get those horses ready for our ride."

This was the first time Rem had been in the barn with a woman by his side other than Callie. So many memories came flooding into his mind. Rem's expression grew serious as he reached for the reins and saddle blanket. Seeing this, Andrea softly touched his arm and said, "Rem, don't fight it, just embrace it. I know you had a thousand special memories here with Callie. Never forget them, and thank the Lord you had that experience in your life. With me, feel free to cry, shout out in anger, or give me that special big smile of yours."

"Thank you so much for understanding and taking the effort to drive out here," Rem replied. "I think it's time you gave me an update on your life. I recall that you were going to ask your husband for a divorce after we left the plane in London."

Andrea looked up and replied, "Yes, that was the plan. However, before I met him at his hotel, the front desk gave me a letter that my husband had left. It said that he knew I was coming to London to ask for a divorce, and he preferred not to see me. The letter contained divorce papers that he had already signed. He wished me a safe trip back home and told me to trash all the clothes he had left and to keep everything else.

"One of the reasons I wanted a divorce was because of how cold and uncaring he had become. I felt like I barely knew him anymore. Looks like I had him pegged just right, since what happened could not have been colder. Rem, I booked a flight home the following morning. To tell you the truth, I don't think I've ever been more at peace than I was on that seven-hour flight home."

Rem threw the saddle blanket on the horse Andrea was going to ride and said, "I'm happy for you. When I first saw you today, I could see the contentment in your face."

As they rode side by side towards the huge cottonwood grove, Rem noticed the look of peace on her face. "For your first time on a horse, you sit in the saddle like an experienced rider. Nice form for a novice."

"Rem, with the sun setting in the sky, the beauty of this place has taken my breath away. Thanks for letting me share this ride with you. It's beautiful up here. I will need to head out soon so I can be ready for this evening's presentation. It isn't polite when the speaker is late."

Rem replied with an endearing smile, "We can head back to the barn, and I will take care of the horses so you can head out right away. Let me ask you this: since your conference is over on Friday, would you have time Saturday to come out for another ride?"

Andrea smiled and said, "I thought you'd never ask. I'll call the airline to book a later flight."

After Andrea had driven away, Rem unsaddled the horses and brushed them down for the night. It felt good to have some company, someone to talk to.

When Andrea arrived on Saturday morning, Rem had prepared a large cowboy breakfast of bacon, eggs, and hash browns. After she parked her car, Rem waved and yelled out for her to come to the house.

Andrea said with a huge smile, "So besides being a cowboy, you are also a short-order cook. It smells wonderful in here. I can't wait to eat."

Andrea wandered into the living room and noticed how cozy it was with the big leather chairs and stone fireplace. The woolen blankets laid over the back of the chairs and the rifles mounted on the wall completing the Western scene as if Remington himself had painted it on canvas.

Rem stepped into the room beside her, following her gaze. Andrea said, "This room takes my breath away. As a psychologist, I could write a paper on who lives here. I can imagine you sitting here on a cold winter night with a fire going. A bowl of popcorn would probably be nearby as you read your philosophy books. This room brings so much peace."

"Andrea, this room is all about me and what I enjoy in life. I'm glad you like it. Now, let's sit down and eat while breakfast is hot."

As Rem and Andrea returned to the kitchen, Rem said, "Andrea, thanks for making the effort to reach out and come out to see me. I know you were hoping Callie would be here, but it just wasn't to be. I hope you can see that I am moving on."

Over breakfast, Rem shared with Andrea about his visit with Callie's sister Beth and how reading Callie's letter had become a turning point in his life.

Andrea listened quietly, then said, "What a blessing Callie gave you, and her sister, too. Knowing what that letter said and that she chose you—well, that had to be the highlight of your life."

Rem nodded, his voice soft as he cleared the dishes. "It was. And it took me a long time to understand my life wasn't over—it was just the end of one life. Once I accepted that, I could start imagining what a new life might look like." He looked out the window, his gaze distant. "I'm still figuring it out."

After a moment, he forced a smile. "If you're ready, novice, let's go saddle up some horses and hit the trail. Actually, you rode so well on Thursday, I think you've earned a horse with a little more get-up-and-go today."

As they rode, the silence between them was comforting, filled with the sounds of hooves and the wind through the grass. Eventually, Andrea spoke, her words unsteady. "Being out here has reminded me there's more to life than I was living with Mr. Ice Man. I spend all my time studying the brain, but it doesn't help me explain the loneliness or what feelings I'm even experiencing."

She looked over at Rem before continuing. "I've been alone a lot. I lost my parents these past few years. My ex tore me apart in ways I'm still trying to understand, and the idea of moving on just… it terrifies me. I haven't even been on a date since the divorce. It's ironic, isn't it? A psychologist not being able to figure herself out."

Rem's voice was quiet but steady. "Sometimes life changes without asking. Good or bad, we don't always get a say. The trick is keeping your heart open for whatever comes next."

Andrea blinked back tears. "You sound like a wise man for a novice psychologist."

He chuckled softly. "Maybe."

By the time they reached the barn, clouds had gathered on the horizon. Andrea brushed her horse down, her hands lingering on the saddle before turning to face Rem. "I guess this is it. My flight… I need to head back."

He walked her to her car, his steps slow, as if prolonging the goodbye might hold off what came after. "Maybe you'll come back out here sometime," he said, forcing a smile that didn't quite reach his eyes.

Andrea hesitated, her voice low. "I'd like that. You were right, you know. About this place. There's something magical about it. It's hard to explain."

Rem pulled off his hat and stepped toward her. He wrapped her in a long embrace, pressing a soft kiss to her forehead. He took her hand and placed the mountain lion's claw into her palm. "I'll tell you about this sometime. For now, keep this and let this remind you not to be angry, not to be unhappy, and to take every day as a blessing from God. Take care of yourself, Andrea," he whispered.

"You too, Rem. Let this place keep healing you."

She stepped into her car, leaving him standing alone in the gravel driveway. As she pulled away, he raised a hand in farewell, the wind lifting his hat slightly as if to remind him he wasn't alone—not really. The ranch stretched behind him, steady and enduring, like the life he was still learning to rebuild.

And as the sun began to break through the clouds, Rem let out a breath and whispered, "One day at a time."

AFTERWORD

So, why do I feel a connection to Robert James Waller? Well, it isn't one where I know the man very well. I compare it to when you see a beautiful girl on the dance floor. With the lights down low, while you can't clearly see her, you swear that you have not only seen her before but also in many different locations over many years.

Robert James Waller, now deceased, was six years older than me. We both grew up in blue-collar families in small towns located about 40 miles apart in northeastern Iowa. His two essay books, *Just Beyond the Fire Light* and *One Good Road Is Enough*, describe in detail what rural life was like for boys growing up in the 1950s. Wow, could I identify. Not only did I enjoy reading his descriptive words of life in those days but also, being from the same general area, I was able to identify with the names of the various rivers for canoeing, marshes for fishing, and Friday night sport rivalries between nearby towns. Waller would tell the stories of Iowa life right down to the wonderful smells of the Maid-Rite food stands and the typical small-town restaurant menu of hot roast beef sandwiches to be served every day at noon. At that time in Iowa, noon was dinner time and supper was served in the evening. With a smile on my face and with that special hometown feeling we all have experienced, I was taken back to my childhood days, a time that Waller and I shared. A time we both cherished and understood.

My first personal connection with Waller came when I was an undergrad at the University of Northern Iowa (UNI), located in Cedar Falls, Iowa, where Waller also attended school. My first interaction with him was when he was a long-haired, guitar-playing singer. As a grad student, he would perform in one of the college bars located on "the Hill" next to the university . . . a place I knew well and referred to as "study hall."

Time passed, and Waller left the university to earn his PhD at the University of Indiana. I was drafted by the United States Army and went on to serve in counterintelligence in Germany. Before leaving for service in the Army, my wife Marcia and I rented a small cabin for three months on the Cedar River just up the road from where Waller and his wife Georgia lived. After serving my stint, I returned to Cedar Falls to enroll in grad school at UNI. Waller had also returned to UNI and was a professor at the UNI Business School.

Years later, as a businessman in Denver, Colorado, I read the book (and saw the movie) *The Bridges of Madison County*, as did 60 million other people. Not only did I love the book, but I was surprised Waller could even write fiction. He was a very well-known scholar who wrote articles on business, economics, mathematics, and the environment.

After reading Waller's second book, *Slow Dance in Cedar Bend*, I felt another strong connection to Waller. Why? Unlike many other readers, I recognized most of the locations described in the book. Earlier, when I said I lived just up the road from Waller on the Cedar River, I meant that I was literally just around the bend. Remember, Waller and I both drove down the same roads, walked the same college hallways, and knew some of the same college professors, deans, and presidents. Believe me when I tell you that many of his fictional characters actually did exist in real life.

This *Slow Dance in Cedar Bend* connection then prompted me to visit the actual bridge located in Madison County, Iowa. This visit helped shed more light on the story of Robert Kincaid and Francesca Johnson, and possibly some insight into the backstory of why *Bridges* was written.

ACKNOWLEDGMENTS

I would like to thank the people who provided help, stories, and review time.

The first readers of my rough manuscript gave of their valuable time and even more so; they gave of their hearts. When I saw them connect so deeply to Rem and Callie, I knew that I must proceed on to tell this story. Thank you, Erin Ward, Brittany Porter, Elly Perry, David Twibell, Bob Miller, Sherri Parrish, Su Ryden, Erik Jensen, and Michelle Brittenham.

I need to make special mention of the person who helped me at the beginning. Pam Lightsey was my sounding board, typist, and more than anything, the female touch to Callie's journals.

After Pam moved to Alaska, Kayla Mulkin, a recent graduate from the University of Colorado at Colorado Springs, provided her screenwriting and technical skills to add finishing touches to the book.

Lisa Pelto, President of Concierge Marketing Inc. in Omaha, Nebraska, provided publishing services that I can only describe as adding the frosting on the cake. I tip my hat and highly recommend her to all authors.

A special thanks to a newfound colleague who feels more like a long-lost brother. Joe Gschwendtner is an amazing man who has broadened my horizons and reinforced the love of accomplishment in life. His input, advice, and friendship were invaluable.

Most importantly, my old cowboy friend provided me with a timeless love story from Douglas County, Colorado. To watch a tough old cowboy in his seventies cry as he recollected the most heartbreaking time in his life gave me the drive to tell this story. Thank you, my friend! I so wish I could tell everyone who you are.

★

Made in the USA
Middletown, DE
30 March 2025